I.S. 61 Library

BETSY BYARS

Bingo Brown, Gypsy Lover

PUFFIN BOOKS

Drawings by Cathy Bobak

PUFFIN BOOKS
Published by the Penguin Group
Viking Penguin, a division of Penguin Books USA Inc.,
375 Hudson Street, New York, New York 10014, U.S.A.
Penguin Books Ltd, 27 Wrights Lane, London W8 5TZ, England
Penguin Books Australia Ltd, Ringwood, Victoria, Australia
Penguin Books Canada Ltd, 10 Alcorn Avenue, Toronto, Ontario, Canada M4V 3B2
Penguin Books (N.Z.) Ltd, 182–190 Wairau Road, Auckland 10, New Zealand

Penguin Books Ltd, Registered Offices: Harmondsworth, Middlesex, England

First published in the United States of America
by Viking Penguin, a division of Penguin Books USA Inc., 1990
Published in Puffin Books, 1992
10
Copyright © Betsy Byars, 1990
All rights reserved

LIBRARY OF CONGRESS CATALOGING-IN-PUBLICATION DATA
Byars, Betsy Cromer.
Bingo Brown, gypsy lover / by Betsy Byars.   p.   cm.
Reprint. Originally published: New York : Viking, 1990.
Summary: A sixth-grade boy deals with the prospect of a new baby
brother and a long-distance love relationship.
ISBN 0-14-034518-3
[1. Babies—Fiction.   2. Brothers—Fiction.]   I. Title.
PZ7.B9836Bic 1992   [Fic]—dc20   91-29177

Printed in the United States of America
Set in Sabon

Contents

Bingo Brown,
Gypsy Lover

Shopper's Block

Bingo Brown had been shopping for a Christmas present for Melissa for four hours, and nothing he had seen was worthy of her. Also, Bingo only had three dollars and thirty-nine cents.

He paused in Belk's fine jewelry department to admire the watches.

"Can I help you?" the clerk asked.

"I wish you could," he answered sadly.

He stumbled on through Scarves and Belts, Hosiery, Cosmetics, staring at the bright merchandise with unseeing eyes.

He was beginning to have a hopeless feeling, as if he were doomed to continue walking through stores for the rest of his life. It was sort of like writer's block, he decided. Writer's block was a mental thing that happened to all writers sooner or later. Writers got to the point where they could not write, not even a word. Bingo had had writer's block twice, so he knew what he was talking about.

Now it seemed to him that he had shopper's block. He could not buy anything, anything! Even if he found the perfect gift—although this did not seem likely—he would not be able to buy it.

He went out into the mall and stood watching little children have their pictures taken with Santa. He briefly considered sending Melissa a photograph of himself on Santa's knee, as a sort of comic present. . . .

This idea told Bingo how low he had fallen. Shaking his head, he made his way toward Sears.

Only this morning, he remembered, he had been a happy person.

A letter from Melissa had come in the mail and, as usual, he got a warm feeling just holding the envelope. If she had just sent the envelope, Bingo had thought, he would be happy.

Actually, after he opened it, he wished she *had* just sent the envelope. The first sentence chilled his bones.

He had been in his room. He always liked to open Melissa's letters in private, because sometimes her letters made his heart pound like a hammer.

Also his face reflected emotions the way a pond ripples at the slightest breeze.

He had closed the door, opened the letter, and read.

He felt his usual thrill when he saw "Dear Bingo." He

loved letters that started that way. Dear Bingo. Whoever had thought that up deserved a medal. Dear Bingo.

Then came the worst sentence he had ever read in his entire life.

"I finished your Christmas present today, and I KNOW you're going to love it."

Bingo threw open the door and stumbled back into the living room. The letter was clutched over his heart.

"Mom!"

"If you are coming in here to ask about the baby—"

"No, no, I'm not."

Bingo's mom was seven and three-thirtieths months pregnant, and she knew whether the baby was a boy or a girl, but she wouldn't tell Bingo or his dad. She wouldn't even give them a hint except, "It's either going to be a boy or a girl."

He and his father had a pact. "If I find out, I'll tell you, and if you find out, you tell me," his dad had said.

Then they had shaken hands like men.

"Mom, a terrible thing has happened."

His mom had her shoes off and her feet up. She was looking through a catalog of baby furniture. "What?"

"You remember Melissa? Out in Bixby, Oklahoma?"

"Yes, I remember Melissa."

"I just found out a terrible, terrible thing—she's giving me something for Christmas."

"How'd you find that out?"

"She told me. Here it is in black and white. 'I finished your Christmas present today and I KNOW—' *know* is in capital letters which means, unfortunately, that it's something nice—'I KNOW you're going to love it.' I'm not just going to like it, Mom, I'm going to *love* it. *Love*'s not underlined but it might as well be."

"So?"

"Mom, this means I have to give her something and it has to be something *she* will love."

"Only if you want to."

"No, Mom, I have to!"

"Send her a Christmas card."

"Mom!" Bingo said, genuinely shocked.

His mom leaned back thoughtfully. "She says she just finished it. That means it's something she made herself."

"Yes, yes. Go on."

His mom sat up. "Oh, Bingo, do you suppose it could be homemade fudge?"

"Of course not."

"Bingo, lately I have just been craving homemade fudge, the kind with real butter. Have you gotten my Christmas present yet?"

"No."

"Well, make me some fudge with real butter."

"I'll make your fudge as soon as I've figured out what to do about Melissa."

"I'm sorry, Bingo. I got diverted. Sit down and read the letter. Maybe there's another clue."

He sank down onto the sofa.

" 'I bought your Christmas present today and I KNOW you're going to love it. Don't feel that you have to give me anything'—"

"See, don't feel you have to give her anything. She says that herself, so don't give her anything. Your problem is solved."

"You didn't let me finish. 'Don't feel that you have to give me anything unless you really want to.' "

"Well, you don't really want to."

"Oh, Mom!" Bingo scanned the letter, looking for clues. He muttered to himself, "Let's see. . . . She's joined a club—the Rangerettes. . . . She's got a new cat—Buffo. . . . She and her best friend are reading a book called *Gypsy Lover,* and every time they get to a good part, she thinks of—" Bingo broke off.

"Well, don't leave me in suspense. Who does she think of when she and her friend get to the good parts of *Gypsy Lover?*"

"No one. It's no one you know."

"Try me. I know a lot of people."

Bingo folded the letter up and put it back in the envelope in a businesslike way.

"Anyway, there are no hints about the gift, none at all. I'll go to my room now."

He walked, head held high, through the door, but as he got to the privacy of his room, he staggered slightly, as if a heavy load had fallen on him, as it had.

He took out the letter and, with a sinking heart, began to read it to himself.

My best friend and I are reading a book
called *Gypsy Lover*. It's a wonderful book.
She reads part, then I read part, and when
I'm reading and I get to a really good part,
instead of going, 'Oh, Romondo,'—that's
the gypsy lover's name, I go, 'Oh, Bingo,'
and my best friend goes, 'I knew you were
going to do that. I knew it! Now read it
right or hand me the book.'

Bingo's eyes rolled up into the top of his head.

Not only did he have to come up with a gift! Not only did the gift have to be something nice! This gift had to be worthy of a gypsy lover!

"Excuse me," Bingo said as he turned from the toy store and bumped into a woman. It would be unthinkable to get Melissa a toy—although he had noticed that yo-yos and Slinkies were on sale.

He ricocheted from the woman directly into a girl. "Excuse me," he said again.

The girl said, "That's okay." Then in a friendlier voice, "Oh, hi."

Bingo stumbled on through the mall. He paused to glance in Hallmark, he walked through a store where everything cost exactly one dollar. He could have gotten Melissa three things in there, but, still in the grip of shopper's block, he made no purchase.

He came to the bookstore. He was now in a daze. He stopped, then surprised himself by turning into the bookstore. His spirits lifted a little.

Did his feet know something his brain did not? Was he going to buy Melissa a book? Was his shopper's block ended? Were there books that only cost three dollars and thirty-nine cents?

"Is there anything I can help you with?" the clerk asked.

Bingo expected to hear himself say something like, "Where are your bargain books?" Instead he heard these words: "Do you happen to have a book called *Gypsy Lover*?"

Wild Reckless Growth

"The romance section is right over there. Do you know the author?"

Bingo shook his head. "No, I just know a girl who's reading it."

"They're arranged alphabetically, by author, so if you knew—"

"No."

Bingo walked to the romance section and stood with his hands behind his back. He scanned titles heavy with passion and lust. He saw a lot of pirates, more than he had expected—he didn't know women went for pirates. He saw enough sea captains to command a fleet. He saw English lords and Arab chieftains. He saw no gypsies.

There had to be gypsies. No romance section should be without gypsies.

Bingo reached out to see if there were any gypsies lurking behind the pirates and sea captains, but his hands never

reached the shelf. For at that moment Bingo noticed something that put gypsies and pirates out of his mind.

His arms were growing! They had grown about four
inches since this morning! They were sticking out of his
jacket sleeves!

He stepped back in alarm. He glanced down at himself.
Nothing else about him was growing—just his arms. He
looked like a scarecrow!

He bent to examine his legs to see if by some miracle
they had grown too. But his pants weren't too short, just
his jacket sleeves.

He looked from one arm to the other. How had he not
noticed that this terrible thing was happening?

He glanced around quickly to see if any shoppers were
aware of his distress. They weren't, and Bingo drew his
arms back into his sleeves to make them less noticeable.
He pulled the cuffs over his wrists.

They still stuck out!

When had this happened? Were his arms continuing to
grow even as he stood here? By the time he got home would
his knuckles be dragging on the ground like an ape?

A voice behind him said shyly, "Hi, Bingo."

He spun around, and immediately realized he could
never spin around again. His arms were like weapons. The
girl was lucky she hadn't been whirled into the book-
shelves.

She said again, "Hi."

It was a girl from school—a new girl, but even if she
had been his oldest and dearest friend Bingo would not

have been able to remember her name at this crucial moment.

"You just bumped into me—didn't you notice—back at the toy store?"

"No, no, but I'm sorry."

"Oh, you already said that," she smiled, "—back at the toy store."

"Oh."

"You looking for a book?" she asked.

"I was . . . I don't know. . . . You'll have to excuse me—I just had a terrible shock."

"What kind of shock?"

"Personal," Bingo said. "It was a personal shock."

"Most of them are."

Bingo clutched the cuffs of his jacket with his fingers and stretched them down. The bones of his wrists were still—as he knew they would be—exposed.

"I thought when I saw you standing over here in romances, that maybe you were buying your mom's Christmas present because, I don't know, you don't seem the type to be reading this kind of book. I would have expected to find you back in something like—" A pause for emphasis. "—science fiction."

He was unable to speak.

"If that's what you were doing," she went on helpfully, apparently unaware of the growth that was occurring inside his sleeves.

And his arms were growing. He could feel it happening at this very moment! The bones were elongating and the flesh and muscles were going right along, stretching like rubber bands—

"If that's what you were doing—shopping for your mom, I could recommend *Wild Reckless Summer*—this one." She touched the picture of a woman with a lot of hair on her head being embraced by a pirate with a lot of hair on his chest. "There's *Wild Reckless Autumn* and *Wild Reckless Winter* and *Wild Reckless Spring*, but my sister says *Wild Reckless Summer* is the best."

At the moment, Bingo was so worried about wild reckless growth that he had no idea what she was babbling about. She might as well have been speaking in Hindu.

"I prefer science fiction myself," she said pointedly, but Bingo didn't get the point. "Somebody told me you write science fiction."

"Excuse me," he said.

"You're leaving?"

"I must."

"You're not going to buy a book?"

"I can't."

"Why not?"

"Oh, well, I came in to look for a book called *Gypsy Lover,* but it doesn't seem to be here."

"I'll help you look."

"No, I don't want it anymore."

"Well . . ."

She sounded hurt, so he turned back to where she stood, framed in the purples and reds and shocking pinks of the romance section—the colors of passion, Bingo thought, though a person with arms like his would probably never have the opportunity to enjoy such colors.

"Thanks anyway, Boots." The name came to him without the help of his brain, and Boots gave him a grateful smile.

" 'Bye, Bingo."

"I appreciate your trying to help."

"Oh, you're welcome."

"And I'm sorry I bumped into you."

"I'm glad you did."

"Good-bye."

He would have waved good-bye if, of course, he had had shorter arms. If he waved with these arms, he'd create a tornado-like wind that would blow all the books from the shelves.

With his arms folded over his chest, his hands tucked into his armpits, Bingo started for the exit.

The Gypsy-Lover Letter

"Mom!"

"What?"

"Look at my arms."

"What's wrong with them?"

"Look!"

"I am looking. I don't see anything wrong."

"Mom, they've grown! Look how long they are. Wait—let me put my jacket back on. There!"

He let his arms stick rigidly out of his jacket sleeves. The cuffs barely covered his elbows.

"So you're growing—you're supposed to grow."

"I'm supposed to grow, but all together! Not in parts! A person's not supposed to grow two long arms and then two adult ears and then size-twelve feet!"

"Bingo—"

"Growing's supposed to be a natural thing that you don't even notice. And what if it keeps on—did you ever stop to think of that? What if my arms keep getting longer and longer, because that's exactly what they feel like they're doing! Then what?"

"Bingo, your arms are fine. I washed the jacket and it probably shrank a little. Now calm down and show me what you bought Melissa."

"I forgot all about Melissa—I couldn't find anything to buy and I kept looking and I still couldn't find anything to buy and I went in the bookstore to—to browse and I noticed how long my arms had gotten and I came home. That was my entire day."

"Sit down, Bingo, relax. Your dad'll be home in a minute and—"

"I wonder if Dad's arms did this?"

"Probably. Oh, listen, we're going out to eat tonight," his mother continued, as if to divert him with a new topic. "You can pick the place, Bingo. Where would you like to go? Only please don't pick Chinese—"

"I'm afraid to eat. The nourishment will go to my arms. I know it will."

"Bingo." She smiled. "Sit down. I have a confession to make."

"What is the confession?"

"Sit down first."

He sat, his long arms slung awkwardly over his knees. He didn't think she really had a confession, she just wanted to try another diversion—as if anything could divert a person whose arms were growing! And just since he got home, they had gotten even—

"I read your letter."

"What?"

"I read your letter."

He was on his feet, diverted.

"I read Melissa's letter."

"Mom!"

"I couldn't help myself. I went in your room to put some clean socks in your drawer and the letter was right there on top of the chest of drawers, open."

"Mom!"

"Actually," she went on, "I only read the part about the gypsy lover. I skipped the part about Buffo and the Rangerettes."

"Mom!" He could only repeat her name, as the shock rolled over him again and again like waves.

She shrugged. "I'm sorry."

"Mom, just because you're pregnant doesn't give you the right to do anything you want."

"I know that."

"No, you don't. Ever since you got pregnant, you've been acting like you are the only person in the family who needs kindness and consideration. You do terrible things and then no one is allowed to do anything terrible back."

"I said I was sorry."

"Yes, but you don't act like it. If you were sorry, you wouldn't be smiling to yourself. What if I went in your room and read your letters?"

"You do that all the time. You read my letters, you read your father's novel. . . ."

"I have to read his novel in case he needs help!"

Bingo and his mom were good arguers and Bingo felt they could keep this one going for days, weeks even. Even a year from now, if she criticized him for something, he would answer, "Well, at least I don't go around reading people's private letters!"

"Like the gypsy-lover letter?" she would answer, and they would be off.

Now she rested one hand on her stomach and smiled. "The baby's moving."

"You claim the baby's moving every time you want to get out of something."

"The baby *is* moving."

She reached out, took Bingo's hand, and laid it on her stomach. Something small and round pushed against his hand. A fist? A foot? He drew in his breath.

"Did you feel it?"

"Oh, yes."

He withdrew his hand and put it in his pocket as if he were depositing something he wanted to save. His mother's smile softened.

"When the baby moves like that—a strong move—it makes me happy. I relax. Sometimes a whole day goes by and the baby doesn't move and I worry."

"Why? Is that something to worry about?"

"Not really, but— Oh, maybe it's because I wasn't happy about the baby at first. Now I want it too much."

"I want it now too."

She said, "Will you forgive me about the letter if I tell you what the baby's going to be?"

"What letter?" he said. It was surprising how the small touch of a baby's hand could push away something like his mother snooping in his mail.

"Melissa's."

"Oh, I forgive you, I guess," he went on with unusual grace. "I have to admit that I do occasionally read secret things myself. Perhaps it's an inherited quality."

"So, do you want to know about the baby?"

"Yes, but you don't have to tell me if you don't want to. I mean, if you want the baby to be a surprise, I'll understand."

"I want to tell you."

"And there's one other thing. Dad and I have a pact—we shook hands on it—that if he found out he would tell me, and if I found out I would tell him."

"It's a little boy, Bingo. His name's going to be Jamie."

"Jamie."

Bingo's heart closed on the word like a fist.

"Yes, James Samuel Brown, for both of your grandfathers. We're going to call him Jamie."

Bingo had a moment of such terrible jealousy that he would not have been surprised to look into a mirror and discover he had turned green, like in cartoons.

He himself had been named by the doctor who had cried capriciously, "Bingo!" as he popped into the world. It was as if his mother had now decided to undo all the mistakes she had made with him. She would name the baby the way babies are supposed to be named—for beloved and dignified relatives.

She would probably then continue and do all the wonderful, loving things that she had not done with him. He would be the imperfect, clumsy older brother, with gorilla arms, while Jamie—

He bet when Jamie came in and said, "Mom, my arms are growing," she wouldn't say, "Oh, they are not." She would leap into action. "I'm getting you to a doctor. We're shortening those arms."

His dark thoughts continued.

And when Jamie fell in love with a girl in Bixby, Oklahoma, she wouldn't say, "Absolutely no more long-distance calls!" She would say, "You can call, but don't talk any longer than two hours."

And when Jamie—

"Oh, here comes your father," his mother said. "Now, don't tell him, Bingo. I want to do it myself."

"No, I won't tell."

"But I want to wait till after supper, all right?"

Bingo said, "Whenever . . ."

One Misery, Extra Large, with Pepperoni

Bingo's father said, "So, Bingo, aren't you going to eat any pizza?"

"What? Oh, sure, Dad, sorry."

"After all, you picked the place."

"Right." Bingo took an unwanted bite of pizza. "I'm not as hungry as I thought I was."

Bingo's mom said, "Bingo's worried because he hasn't been able to come up with a Christmas present for Melissa."

"That's one of the things I'm worried about," Bingo admitted.

"How much do you have to spend?"

"Three dollars—and change."

"Send her a rose."

"A what?"

"A rose. I always had great success with a single rose."

"Not with me," his mother interrupted.

"That's why you hardly ever get roses anymore. Now I have to save up until I have enough for a dozen." His father turned back to Bingo. "You could get one rose for fifty cents back then. I suppose they're more now, and of course you'll have to pay to have the florist deliver it. Where does the girl live?"

"You know . . . Bixby, Oklahoma."

"Yes, that'll cost you."

Bingo didn't have the heart to tell his father a single rose might have been all right in olden days when girls pressed flowers in books and fainted at Elvis Presley concerts. Today, girls read *Gypsy Lover* and had given up fainting entirely.

Yes, he was definitely on his own as far as Melissa's present was concerned.

Bingo's dad took a bite of pizza and returned the slice to his plate. There was a long string of melted cheese from Bingo's dad's mouth to his plate, and his dad wound it around one finger and put it in his mouth.

"So what are your other problems?" he said then, licking his finger. "Anything else I can help you with? I'm in the mood to solve problems."

"No. . . . Nothing." Bingo looked down at his own pizza. "It doesn't matter."

His mom said, "He thinks his arms are growing."

"Mom! I don't *think*, they *are* growing. I can feel them growing. If you'd bother to look, you could actually see them gro—"

"Bingo!" His dad reached out and took Bingo by the shoulder.

"What, Dad? What is it?"

"I just remembered that when I was about your age, my ears did that."

"What?"

"Grew! And the darn things did it overnight. One night I went to bed and my ears were normal, well, as normal as ears can be, and the next morning I got up and looked in the mirror and I was Dumbo. I had these huge ears, huge! And I had not had them the night before—I knew I hadn't."

"What did you do?"

"Well, the first thing I did was stagger back to bed. This in itself was a miracle because I had almost passed out in the bathroom from shock—and my mom came in. She said, 'What is wrong with you this time?' She always said, 'this time,' as if to imply that things happened often enough to become burdensome.

"I couldn't even answer. I just pointed to my ears. She saw the ears, of course, she had to, but she pretended to think I had a hearing defect. 'WHAT IS WRONG WITH YOU THIS TIME?' she yelled.

"I said, 'Mom, Mom, my ears are growing.' My mother—she doesn't look strong now, but Bingo, back then she was as strong as a dockworker. She jerked me out of bed and made me get dressed. She used physical force. She could hardly get my sweatshirt over my head—that's how big my ears were!

"The day before, this exact same sweatshirt had slipped right over my head, but now it caught on these huge ears and my mother had to yank and yank and yank and still she pretended nothing was wrong.

"Of course, maybe she was pretending not to notice in order to get me out of the house so she could pass out from shock herself, in private, but . . . still . . . still . . ." He trailed off.

"So how did your ears get back to normal?"

"They never did. These are them." He turned his head from side to side.

"I know how you guys feel," his mother said, smiling. "I get the feeling my stomach's growing."

"Mom."

Bingo gave her a withering look. He wished she would learn that jokes are unwelcome in the middle of serious conversations.

He turned back to his father, "But, Dad, arms are different from ears. You can measure their growth by your sleeves so there can't be any mistake about how—"

Bingo's mom reached out and put her hand around his dad's wrist, like a bracelet, causing him to look at her. "Oh, Sam," she said with unusual gentleness, "I was going to save the news until after supper, but I just can't. I'm too happy."

"What?"

"I already told Bingo."

"Told him what?"

She rested one hand on the curve of her stomach. "It's a little boy."

"A boy?"

"Yes."

"A boy!"

Bingo thought his dad looked like a light bulb had gone on inside him.

"A son." His father breathed the word.

"Like me," Bingo said, looking from one parent to the other in amazement. "That's what's sitting at the table with you right now. A son. I am a son. The very thing that is now blissing you out is here! And has been here for over twelve years. Me! I am—"

Now his mom encircled Bingo's wrist tightly, silencing him.

"I'm going to name him James Samuel, for our fathers," she said. "We're going to call him Jamie."

Gyps

"Remember this?"

Bingo's mother was decorating the Christmas tree. She held up a Santa Claus Bingo had made in nursery school.

Santa's body was wrapped in red yarn, but beneath the yarn was obviously the cardboard from a roll of toilet paper. The cotton beard had always been skimpy—Bingo had been absent when the cotton was passed out and had had to depend on donations from fellow classmates. Now the cotton was gray and was coming unglued. The cotton eyebrows were missing entirely.

"Oh, Mom, throw that thing away."

"It's my favorite ornament."

"Then you have very poor taste."

He started to head for his room and his mother said casually, "Oh, by the by."

Bingo stopped.

His mother always said, "Oh, by the by," in that casual

way when she was getting ready to pull the rug out from under him. His shoulders tightened as if to steel himself for the blow.

"What?"

"A girl called while you were out."

Bingo couldn't help himself. He whirled. "Was it long-distance?"

"No, sorry, Gyps, just a local call."

Bingo stopped breathing. He froze like ice. The only sign that he was still living was that his eyes narrowed.

"*What* did you call me?"

"Oh, nothing," his mother said with a smile. She went back to trimming the tree. "Oh, here's another of my favorites."

She held up the pinecone reindeer he had made in kindergarten. The left pipe-cleaner antler was missing, and the reindeer dangled, tilting drunkenly to the right.

Bingo was not diverted. "Oh, yes, you did. You called me 'Gyps.' Don't deny it. I heard you."

His mother hung the reindeer on a branch. She regarded it critically, and then tried to center the lone antler. "Now we have a unicorn reindeer. Maybe there's a song in that. Rudolph, the unicorn reindeer—"

"Don't try to change the subject, because it won't work. You distinctly called me 'Gyps.' "

"Well, if I did do it, I did it for a joke, Bingo."

"I do not find it funny."

"I was teasing."

"I do not like to be teased."

"Well, I won't do it anymore."

"It's bad enough that you read my mail—"

His father called from the bedroom, "That's enough, Bingo."

"Dad, she deliberately read my mail, which was privileged information, and now she is using it against me!"

"That—is—enough."

"Well, she started it by calling me 'Gyps.' "

"And I'm finishing it."

"Just because she's getting a new child," he muttered as he went to his room, "that does not give her the right to be cruel to the old one."

"Bingo—"

"What do you want?"

"Come here a minute."

Bingo went and stood in the doorway to his parents' room. His dad was at the typewriter, his long freckled fingers resting on the keys.

"What is it, Dad?"

"I want you to be more considerate of your mother."

"Well, I want her to be more considerate of me."

They looked at each other. Bingo felt as if he were being taken apart and put back together and his father had found a few parts defective.

Bingo sighed. "I'll try," he said.

"That's all I'm asking."

"Can I go now?"

"Go. . . . Stay. . . . Do whatever you want."

Bingo went to his room and shut the door firmly behind

him. The letter he had started to Melissa was face-up on his desk. His mother had probably read that too. So far, all there was to read was 'Dear Melissa,' but he still didn't want her seeing it. Somehow, some way she would taunt him with it.

Did all pregnant women taunt their children? he wondered. Was it a trait of pregnancy, like wanting certain foods? If so, it was surprising that pregnancies were still tolerated in the civilized world.

Bingo wadded up the letter and threw it into the trash can.

There was a knock at his window. "I'm not here, Wentworth," Bingo called.

"You may not be *all* there, Worm Brain, but I need to talk to you. I got a problem."

"Join the club."

The knock came again, louder. Tiredly Bingo went to the window. He raised the window about two inches.

"What do you want? Get on with it. Cold air's coming in."

"You remember that girl—Cici?"

"Yes, I remember Cici," Bingo said.

Billy Wentworth had fallen in love with Cici one day in Bingo's backyard. He had introduced himself handsomely with the words, "My name is Willy Bentworth," but the love remained unrequited. Bingo had a lot of respect for that word—"unrequited"—because as soon as you saw it or heard it, even if you didn't know what it meant, you knew you didn't want it to happen to you.

Billy Wentworth was saying, "Well, I need to know if she's giving me something for Christmas."

"Probably not."

"Why do you say that?"

"She can't stand the sight of you, Wentworth. Why would she give you a Christmas present?"

"How do you know she can't stand the sight of me? Just because she, well, avoids me, doesn't mean she can't stand the sight of me. She could be playing hard to get, couldn't she?"

Bingo shook his head.

"Why not?"

"Wentworth, she's not playing hard to get, she's playing impossible to get."

Wentworth continued thoughtfully, "So maybe the thing to do is to get her something and then if she gives me something, I can give her the something that I got for her."

"Good thinking."

"Just one more thing." He paused. "What could I get?"

"Good-bye, Wentworth."

It was hard to slam a window shut when it was only open two inches, but Bingo managed it nicely.

A Brother's Heart

"Bingo!"

Bingo was in his bedroom, standing in the middle of the room. There was a package in his hand. The postmark read Bixby, OK. This package contained Bingo's present from Melissa.

Fifteen minutes ago, Bingo had been in the kitchen, happily reading the recipe for old-timey fudge. He had his apron on, the bowl was out. The measuring spoons clinked pleasantly as he jiggled them in one hand.

Then the doorbell rang. "Coming!" Bingo called cheerfully. He went to the door, the postman said, "Package," and put this box in Bingo's hand.

That had happened fifteen minutes ago, and for fifteen minutes Bingo had been frozen in time, unable go forward or backward. He could not bring himself to open the present, and yet he couldn't reverse time and say to the postman, as he should have, "I'm sorry, but there is no one by the name of Bingo at this address."

Now he was stuck with this package the way people in fairy tales are stuck with curses. If only he had sent something days ago—even the rose. Because as soon as he saw what was in this package, then his choices would narrow. If Melissa had sent him a sweater—and it could be a sweater because girls did knit sweaters—then he would have to send something as good as a sweater.

What was as good as a sweater? A blouse? Didn't blouses come in sizes and didn't girls get offended if you sent something too big?

If only it could be cookies, then he could double the recipe and send fudge. Fudge was like cookies, wasn't it? But would Melissa be ashamed to say, "My boyfriend made me some fudge for Christmas"?

Anyway, it wasn't cookies, because it didn't rattle. It was some sort of garment. He bent the package, testing it. Some sort of—

"Bingo! Bingo, where are you?"

His mother appeared in the doorway.

"Bingo, I got it!"

"What?"

If he had not been frozen in time, he would have hidden the package behind his back or thrown it under the bed, out of the range of his mother's scorn. Now she would pounce on the package like a dog on a bone, and she wouldn't stop until she had seen the gift with her own—

"The fetal stethoscope! I got it!"

She waved the stethoscope in the air, and it jiggled as if it had come alive. Bingo remembered how at the beach she had once pulled up a huge crab and waved it in the same carefree way.

"Come on! Bingo, you can hear Jamie's heart! I stopped by Mom's on the way home and she listened and said it sounded like an old Maytag washer she used to have. Come on! Tell me what you think."

She went into the living room. "Aren't you coming?" she called over her shoulder.

"Yes, but first I have to do something with this—this thing I got in the mail today."

"That can wait. I have to have the stethoscope back by six."

He went into the living room with the package under his arm. He would have liked to hide it, but the package seemed somehow attached to him. Would he ever be able to open it, he wondered, or would he carry it through life, always wondering, worrying—

"Come on, Bingo!"

His mother was on the sofa, the stethoscope against the curve of her stomach.

"There it is," she said softly.

She handed him the ends of the stethoscope. Bingo had to put down his package in order to take them. He couldn't release the package, of course, because of the curse, so he stuffed it between his knees.

Bingo hated to do that because now his mother was sure to notice he was standing knock-kneed and then she would notice the reason for the knock-knees and then she would say, "Why is that package between your knees?"

"Can you hear it?" she asked.

"I hear something like stomach noises, sort of a gurgling sound."

"No, that's not it. Wait." She paused to shift the stethoscope. "There. Try that."

He listened and she watched for his expression.

"Can you hear it?"

Ta-da-dum   ta-da-dum   ta-da-dum   ta-da-dum   ta-da-dum—

"Oh, yes."

"What does it sound like to you, Bingo?"

"Like a heart, I guess. This is the first heart I ever heard. Ta-da-dum ta-da-dum, like that."

The beat was steady, rhythmic, but Bingo's own heart began to race with emotion. He closed his eyes.

He did not understand the intensity of his feeling as he listened to his brother's heart. Maybe it was listening to a small heart that was sort of practicing, getting ready for the day when it would have to pump for real—to race with emotion or slow or flutter or do whatever it had to to keep up with the unexpectedness of life.

Or maybe there was some sort of brotherly tie that bound, like in literature where the Corsican brothers felt each other's joy and pain or where—

He opened his eyes. His mother was smiling up at him. "Oh, Bingo, I want this little baby so much."

"I do too."

"Now, let me listen to your heart. I've never heard your heart, Bingo."

"My heartbeat won't be anything special. It's just regular. However . . ." He raised his sweatshirt to reveal his chest.

"That's the way heartbeats are supposed to be—regular." She raised up on one elbow. "Oh, there's the phone. Get that, will you, Bingo?"

"Sure."

"If it's your dad tell him to come home before six so he can listen to Jamie's heart. Then stick around so I can listen to yours."

Bingo removed Melissa's package from between his knees. He had forgotten about it. The emotional moment of hearing his brother's heart had caused his knees to clamp together and the package had suffered a serious cave-in as a result.

Bingo carried the package with him to the phone. "Hello?"

His mother had the stethoscope in her ears again, listening, smiling faintly.

A girl's voice said, "Bingo?"

"Yes."

"Bingo Brown?"

His mother raised up on one elbow. "Is it your dad?"

"No."

"Who is it?"

"I don't know! The conversation hasn't started yet."

He could tell from his mother's expression that when it did start, she was aware it would be a mixed-sex one.

"Bingo?"

"Yes."

"This is Boots. Do you remember me? I was the girl in the mall—remember the day something terrible happened to you?"

Boots—this was the girl who had interrupted him while his arms were growing. "Oh, yes, the bookstore."

"Well, you may have forgotten all about this, but you mentioned you wanted a book called *Gypsy Lover* and, Bingo, guess what? My sister has it!"

Bingo/Romondo

Boots said, "Bingo, did you hear what I just told you?"

"Yes, yes, I heard."

"You don't sound excited."

"Well, you caught me by surprise," Bingo said. He began to fan himself with Melissa's package.

"It's one of my sister's very, very favorite books. She's read it so many times, it, like, falls open at the good parts. Wait a minute, I'll make it fall open."

"Oh, no, you don't have to do that."

On the sofa, Bingo's mother had abandoned all pretenses of listening to fetal heartbeats. She was watching him with one of her smiles.

"I want to. Oh! It did it on its own. Wait a minute, I have to check for the good part." There was a pause. "Okay, here it is. Are you ready for this?"

Bingo told the truth. "Not really." But Boots began to read anyway.

"Romondo's lips curled into a slow, lazy smile, but his dark eyes, staring at her across the campfire, had deepened with longing.

"The music of the gypsies seemed to have deepened with longing, too, and couples began to drift off, arm in arm, to their wagons.

"Finally she and Romondo were alone. He put down his guitar and in one flu-id-ly—"

Boots paused to say, "I had to sound that word out—sorry.

"—in one fluidly graceful move was at her side. In a low voice she murmured, 'Romondo.' "

She paused to catch her breath, and Bingo had been waiting for just such a pause. He broke in quickly with, "Thank you so much for, er, sharing that with me."

"Wait. It gets better."

"I—"

"Romondo murmured, 'Marianna.' " Boots broke off to say, "Am I pronouncing that right or should it be MariAHna? That's better—don't you think, because she's a countess. MariAAAHna."

Bingo took a deep breath to calm himself. His heart was pounding in his throat. He couldn't let his mother listen to his heart now. When she found out it was in his throat, she would demand to know why. "Boys' hearts don't jump up into their throats for no reason, young man, now you sit right down here and tell me—"

He cleared his throat. In a new, surprisingly mature voice he said, "I'm sorry, Boots, I don't think that's the book I was looking for."

"Boots!" his mother snorted.

He gave her a withering glance, but, as usual, she refused to wither. She grinned and turned the stethoscope toward him as if to listen in on the conversation.

"It has to be, Bingo. There couldn't possibly be two *Gypsy Lover*s," Boots said.

"Perhaps I had the title wrong."

"No, I remember the title. You said *Gypsy Lover*. And this book is *Gypsy Lover*. If you don't believe this book is *Gypsy Lover*, I can come right over and show you it's *Gypsy Lover*!"

Boots's voice had risen, and she was punching home the title with such force Bingo was afraid the words would reach his mother across the room. It was bad enough that his own words were reaching her. He pressed the receiver against his ear to smother the *Gypsy Lover*s.

"No, no, I do believe that the title of that book is—is the title you just said."

"What was your gypsy lover's name?" she asked.

A low gypsyish voice trilled *Rrrromondo* in his brain, but his mouth stuttered uncertainly, "I—I—"

"Romondo doesn't ring a bell?" She paused. "How about MariAHna?"

"Er, I wonder if I might call you back," Bingo said.

"Well, yes, I guess so, but if it's definitely not the same book, there's no need. I can't believe this. I go to all the

trouble of finding this book and calling you up and let-
ting it fall open to a good part and reading it out loud
and—"

"I appreciate those things. Most people don't go to
enough trouble."

"I could just cry."

"No, no, please don't, because I have to go do a—"
Bingo broke off to think of something he could claim he
had to do. "—an errand. And I couldn't go do this, er,
errand if you're going to—" He turned his back on his
mother. "—to do that."

Boots paused.

"Please," he said.

"Oh, all right, I won't."

"Thank you very much, and I'll be in touch."

In one fluidly graceful movement of his own, Bingo hung
up the telephone and disappeared into his room.

"Bingo, come back here," his mother called.

But Bingo, who sat fanning himself with Melissa's package, did not answer.

The Nightmare with Handles

It was midnight. Bingo was not asleep, and Bingo knew that he would never sleep again, not as long as Melissa's package lay unopened on his dresser.

Bingo got up and crossed the room without a sound. He eased his door shut. There was a faint click as the latch caught, and Bingo waited, frozen, for one of his parents to call, "Bingo, are you still up?"

Nothing happened, and so after a moment Bingo turned on the light. Then he crossed the room and reached for the package.

Bingo had stared at this package so often that he knew every wrinkle in the paper—it had been wrapped in a brown Bi-Lo grocery bag and there was a grease stain beside the postmark. The words DO NOT OPEN TILL CHRISTMAS went around the package like a decorative border in bold Magic Marker letters, but Bingo knew that for the sake of his mental health he had to disregard this message.

If ever he was to close his eyes in sleep again—he would have to open this package and face whatever was inside.

He eased off the Bi-Lo bag covering—no sound must alert his parents to what he was doing—and lifted out the package. The inner wrapping paper was blue with snowmen involved in wintry activities—sledding, ice-skating, and opening packages that contained useful objects like scarves.

Bingo forced himself to stop watching the snowmen— this was stalling, he reminded himself firmly, he had never before shown the slightest interest in what snowmen did in their off-hours. He then forced himself to loosen the tape on either end, forced himself to pull up the flaps, forced himself to take out the box.

The box was also decorative, but Bingo did not pause to see what was on it. Like a man with a mission, he lifted the lid. Manfully, he reached inside. With trembling fingers he lifted Melissa's gift to the light.

Then a cry escaped from Bingo's throat. He didn't even know he had cried out. He turned the object over, and another cry burst from him. A third cry might have followed if Bingo's mother had not thrown open the door.

"Bingo, what's wrong?"

"Mom—"

"What happened? Are you all right? Did you have a nightmare?"

"I wish it were a nightmare."

"What is it? Tell me."

"Mom, oh, Mom—"

She wrapped her robe around her stomach and sank down beside him on the bed. Her hair was pulled back in a ponytail so the light fell directly onto her face, highlighting her concern.

"Mom, I opened Melissa's present."

"What?"

"I got this present from Melissa—" He paused to swallow. "—and I opened it—Mom, I really dreaded opening it—don't ask me why I dreaded opening a package but it's just my nature to dread some things that other people do not dread. If there is some sort of phobia about dreading to open packages then I may have that." He swallowed again. "At any rate I forced myself to open it and finally I did open it and I looked inside and saw—I saw this."

He held up Melissa's gift. His mother stared at it without comprehension. She looked from the present into Bingo's face.

"Mom," he explained, "it is a piece of cloth with handles on it. I was prepared for anything—a book, a T-shirt, a wristwatch—anything but a piece of cloth with handles on it. Mom, what is this?"

His mom looked at it. "Bingo—"

"What?"

"Bingo, it is a piece of cloth with handles on it."

"Mom, Mom, don't try to be funny. Not now, please, not now when I'm desperate."

"I'm not trying to be funny. I'm stating a fact. It's a piece of cloth with handles on it. For some reason Melissa has sent you a piece of cloth with handles."

At that moment Bingo's father appeared in the doorway. He braced his hands on either side of the door. He was framed like a photograph of an unwilling subject. "What is going on here?"

"Sam, look at this. Now, Bingo, don't give your father a hint. Let *him* tell *us* what—"

"It is after twelve o'clock at night," Bingo's dad interrupted. He frowned at his watch and then at them. "You are supposed to be asleep. A pregnant woman needs her sleep. And, Bingo, I asked you to be more considerate of your mom."

"Oh, Sam, I wasn't asleep. My back was hurting again. Now!" She held up the piece of cloth, pulling it apart by the handles as if it were an accordion. "Now! What do you think that is?"

"Maybe you two like to play games at twelve o'clock at night, but you two don't have to get up and go to work at seven."

"Sam, we need your input. It's like that game show where the celebrities have to guess strange objects. You're so good at that. Please."

Bingo's dad sighed. "Well, I had a back scrubber that had handles like that—only it had bristles so that when you scrubbed . . ." He trailed off.

Bingo's mom said, "It could be a tote bag, if it were sewed up on the sides."

"She wouldn't give me a back scrubber or a tote bag!" Bingo said. "Now stop making fun of Melissa's present."

"If Melissa had not wanted us to make fun of her present

then she shouldn't have sent you a piece of cloth with handles on it," his mother said.

"Give it back, please," Bingo said coldly. He reached for the gift and knocked the box onto the floor. A note fluttered out.

Bingo picked up the note and, without considering the consequences, began to read aloud.

"Dear Bingo, you may be wondering what this is. Well, it's a—"

Bingo broke off and folded the note.

"Well, don't stop now. It's a what?"

"Nothing, Mom."

"Listen, you got me up out of bed with hoarse cries of anguish and—"

"Not hoarse cries of anguish. I went, 'Oh,' like that."

"An 'Oh' like that wouldn't have awakened me from a peaceful sleep which I—"

"You said you weren't asleep. You said your back hurt. You—"

Bingo's father said, "Bingo, your mother is not going back to bed until you tell her what that thing is. Now tell her so we can all get some sleep."

"Oh, all right." Then he added in a low voice, "It's a notebook holder."

There was a short silence. Then his mother said, "Bingo Brown! Do you honestly expect me to believe that thing is a notebook holder?"

"It is! Melissa knows I keep notebooks and so she made this for me to keep them in. Wait!"

He went to his drawer and pulled out two of his note-books. "See, you put the notebooks in here and here." He inserted the notebooks. "Then you fold it over and carry it by these. In the note, there are instructions, also a sort of diagram."

He turned the note around. In Melissa's diagram he wore a dignified suit and appeared to be holding a businessman's briefcase. In the mirror beyond, he saw a more realistic picture. There, he wore short, wrinkled pajamas and appeared to be holding a ladies' purse.

His parents regarded him without expression. They sometimes did this just before they exploded into laughter, which, to be honest, Bingo felt they now had every right to do.

Bingo was very grateful that his mother limited herself to, "Well, I guess it could be a notebook holder."

His father sighed and said, "Can we go back to bed now?"

Bingo said, "Please."

His mother went out the door, but Bingo's dad paused

in the doorway. "Bingo, do you think you'll be getting other presents from girls this year?"

"I hope not," Bingo said sincerely.

"So do I, but if you do, try to open them during daylight hours."

"Oh, I will."

"Good night, son."

"Good night."

Bingo waited a moment, listening to see if his parents were holding their explosion of laughter until they were in the privacy of their bedroom. But the house remained quiet. Bingo turned out his light.

Sometimes, to Bingo's surprise, he found he actually loved his parents.

A Bingo Letter Holder

Bingo had not read all of Melissa's note to his parents, and he was glad his parents had not pressed him to do so. Melissa's note was far too personal for any ears or eyes other than his own.

Bingo had read the note seven times. He had read it three times in a row last night, and he had read it four separate times this morning. The note seemed to improve with each reading.

Bingo was going over it in his mind as he pedaled to K Mart. He knew it by heart now.

> Dear Bingo,
>   You may be wondering what this is. Well, it's a notebook holder. I invented it and sewed it myself. What it is is a place to put your notebooks.

At first Bingo had, as a writer, been bothered by two

is's in a row, back to back like that, but now he was beginning to like them.

> See, Bingo, you really are going to be-
> come a great writer one day. I know that.
> And your notebooks will be valuable. Only
> sometimes valuable things get thrown out
> by accident. I know this from personal ex-
> perience.
>
> Last week Mom threw out your letters,
> and it really hurt me, Bingo. My mom saw
> the letters on the floor of my room, by my
> bed, and the reason they were on the floor
> by my bed was because I always read them
> the last thing before I go to sleep. My mom
> was in a very bad mood and she also threw
> out a pair of my brother's favorite socks.
> She said, "In this house, anything on the
> floor is trash. Remember that from now on."
>
> Bingo, please write me some more letters
> and I promise you they will never get
> thrown out. The reason I can promise is be-
> cause I am making a letter holder to keep
> them safe, like I did for your notebooks.
>
> Take care of your notebooks and of your-
> self and write me some letters. Now you have
> a special reason—to fill my letter holder.
>
> > Love,
> > Melissa

Bingo loved this letter. It was the best one Melissa had ever written him. He had already answered it, and the answer was in his back pocket.

Dear Melissa,

I hope you won't be mad with me, but I opened your present. For personal reasons which I won't go into—I don't want to bore you with my troubles at Christmas—I just couldn't wait.

I didn't know what the gift was at first, but that was because it was your own personal invention. I imagine if Alexander Graham Bell had sent someone a telephone, they would have been puzzled too. But as soon as I read your letter, I got my notebooks and put them inside. I showed my parents how it worked. They had, of course, never seen such a thing before either.

I'll get your gift in the mail as soon as I can. I hope you'll enjoy it, although it will never compare with your extraordinary gift to me.

Love and gradidute,
Bingo

Bingo was proud of that word *extraordinary*, because it was the first time he had used it in connection with a gift. Then at the last moment, just as he was folding the letter to put it in the envelope, he discovered he had misspelled *gratitude,* but by crossing the *d* and putting a small loop at the base of the *t,* that was corrected.

Melissa's note and the notebook holder had given him new manliness just at the moment when he needed it most. He now had the courage to go to K Mart where he was sure not only that he would find a gift, but a gift worthy of Melissa, a gift which would, unlike the shabby things he had seen at the mall, be perfect. Bingo could hardly wait to see it himself.

He entered K Mart confidently and walked past the carts—he sensed instinctively that Melissa's gift would not need to be pushed around the store.

He walked past the scarves and umbrellas, ignoring them, also purses and luggage. It was like that old game of Hot and Cold. An internal thermostat was now saying to Bingo, "You're warm. You're getting warmer. You're red-hot! You're burning up! You're on fire!"

Bingo looked around. He now stood in Jewelry.

He took a deep breath. He was directly in front of a counter of miscellaneous jewelry. A sign above warned ALL SALES FINAL.

At first Bingo could not figure out why his inner being had stopped him here. The sale items were depressing— sprung barrettes on soiled cards, dingy plastic bracelets, frayed hair ribbons, strings of beads so snarled together it would have taken centuries to untangle them, tarnished silver jewelry boxes—

And then he saw them. For one electric moment Bingo could not move, could not breathe, could not even reach out his hand. They lay like gems on a pile of trash. It was as if they were wrapped already, with a card on top bearing the name "Melissa."

Earrings. Golden earrings.

He picked them up.

The earrings were small, not too pretentious or gypsyish for a girl of Melissa's age. Indeed, Bingo thought, these earrings would be in good taste for a person of any age, any social standing. And—he gasped aloud at this—they cost fifty-nine cents.

He was so astonished that his first impulse was to find a salesperson and demand if this could possibly be correct. Fifty-nine dollars seemed more like it for earrings like these.

No salesperson was available, however, so Bingo—trusting to luck—proceeded to Christmas Cards. He selected one that said—this had thrilled him too, "Christmas is a Time for Love"—and inside was—"and Lovers."

Inside was, also, a picture of two reindeer embracing, as best they could, and Melissa would like that. She would be surprised, as he had been, about how ardent reindeer can appear.

He paid for his items and pedaled to the post office. He waited at the table behind a businessman who was sorting through some important mail. When the man was through, Bingo stepped up and took the post office pen. He had always wanted a reason to use this pen.

On the inside of the card he wrote, "Well, here they are, Melissa. I hope you like them. I wish I could see your ears with them in them."

He regretted that "them in them." It wasn't really top-notch writing. But the post office pen didn't erase.

He added:

> Merry Christmas forever,
> Bingo

Bingo removed the price tag containing the ridiculous price of fifty-nine cents and inserted the earrings in the Christmas card. He sealed the flap, addressed it with the post office pen, bought two stamps, one for his letter and one for his present, and dropped them through the slot.

As they slipped out of sight, Bingo had an especially cheerful thought. Now Melissa would have two items for her Bingo Letter Holder—a card and a letter.

Then, with a smile on his face and a song in his heart, Bingo got on his bicycle and started for home.

Bad Tidings

Bingo was whistling "Jingle Bells." He was almost home, pedaling his bike in a brisk, carefree way. With every mile, his heart seemed to grow lighter. Bingo was a free man at last.

He was so full of Christmas spirit he thought he would pop open like a piñata and sprinkle the neighborhood with goodies.

He finished "Jingle Bells" and went immediately into "White Coral Bells"—a bell medley, he thought. He felt even better. He put his hands in his pockets and coasted down a hill.

There was nothing, he realized, for raising a man's spirits like selecting the perfect gift for the perfect girl.

Of course, he reminded himself, there was the faint, faint chance that other girls might come across with gifts—Cici and Boots, for example, but he would be ready. Receiving a piece of cloth with handles on it had left him immune to future shocks, the way serum prepares one to resist disease. Never again would he cry out hoarsely—that was his mother's exaggeration, of course—cry out over a gift. Anything he got he would take like a man.

Also, he now knew what to choose for girls. Of course there were no more golden earrings in that sale pile, but there might be other possibilities.

Bingo was whistling "The Bells of St. Mary's" as he put his bicycle in the garage and entered the house.

"Mom!" he called. He shut the door behind him. "Mom, where are you? You are going to be very proud of me. Mom?"

His mother didn't answer.

Bingo went into the kitchen. There was no sign she'd been making her Christmas specialty—rum balls. She hadn't even started supper. Maybe this would be a good time to make another attempt on the old-timey fudge.

He leaned on the sink. Her car had been in the garage, though, so she was bound to be around somewhere.

Bingo checked the bedroom and went back into the living room.

"Mom!"

He saw there was a note stuck under the VCR. This was where the family left messages for each other. He should have noticed it when he first came in, but he was so filled with peace and goodwill that—

He read the note.

Bingo, I'm taking your mom to the hospital—hope it's a false alarm—I'll call when I know something—Dad.

Bingo stopped breathing. He read it again. The short rushed sentences hit him so hard, he had to sit down in a chair.

He read the note a third time.

This third reading left him short of breath. He felt as if he needed to do something like sit down in a chair, but he had already done that.

He went over the note again, word by word, trying to find something there that he hadn't seen before. The words were the kind that would say the exact same thing no matter how many times you read them, no matter where you placed the emphasis, no matter how slowly or how—

The phone rang.

Bingo reached for it so quickly he knocked the receiver to the floor. He pulled it up by the cord.

He said, "Dad?"

"No, Harrison, it's Grammy," his grandmother's voice answered.

Bingo's grandmother was the only person who called him by his real name—Harrison. Usually he liked it. It was refreshing. But now, for the first time, he didn't. Harrison had a formal sound. It was the name someone official would use before delivering bad news.

He rushed in with, "Grammy, Dad's taken Mom to the hospital."

"I know. I was calling to make sure you had gotten the message."

"Yes, I got it."

The note was still in his hand, trembling like a leaf. He put it down beside the phone.

"What happened?"

"Your mom started having pains about noon. She called the doctor and he said for her to come to the hospital. I'm sure the only reason he had her come to the hospital instead of the office is because that's where he happened to be."

"She shouldn't be having pains, should she?"

"No, but it happens sometimes."

"But it's too soon. Pains weren't—pain wasn't supposed to happen for weeks—months. . . . Mom's just—" He paused. "She's just a little over seven and one-fourths months pregnant."

"I know. I've been keeping track of it myself."

"So, it's way too soon!"

"Bingo, we just have to hope for the best. It's not like the old days. They have drugs now—ways to stop premature deliveries. I'm glad she is in the hospital. At least she'll be where they can do something for her."

"I don't want anything to happen to Mom."

"Nothing's going to happen to her."

"Or the baby."

"Bingo—"

"I want to go to the hospital. I want to know what's happening."

"No, Bingo—"

"If you don't want to go, drive me."

"Bingo, our being there will not help at this point. We'd just be in the way."

"Or I'll go on my bike."

"Bingo, I've got a friend in Admittance, and I'm getting ready to call her. She'll know if your mom's going to be admitted. If she is, I'll call you right back."

"I don't want to just sit here."

"Bingo, your mother could be on her way home right now."

"Oh, I hope so."

"And if she has been admitted, I'll come over and we'll wait together—maybe go out to eat."

"I couldn't eat if she's been admitted."

"Well, then we'll just do whatever we feel like doing—hang out."

Bingo didn't answer.

"Now you wait to hear from me."

He still didn't answer.

"Bingo, don't do anything foolish."

"I won't do anything foolish," he said, emphasizing the last word.

He hung up the phone and sat slumped in his chair, his hands dangling between his knees. He had never heard the house so silent. The only sound was the faint whisper of an occasional pine needle falling from the tree onto the presents below.

Bingo couldn't stand to wait any longer. He picked up the phone and dialed his grandmother's number. The line was busy.

Bingo twisted with impatience. He sat sideways in the chair, facing the door.

What was taking his grandmother so long? She'd had time to talk to everybody in the whole hospital, hadn't she?

He hung up the phone and sat in the oppressive silence. It was as if a different, heavier air mass now existed in the living room. This was certainly not the fresh, pine-scented air he had inhaled on his arrival.

How could anybody survive on this thick stuff?

And why didn't his grandmother call?

Maybe *she* was trying to call *me* when I was trying to call *her*.

Immediately Bingo picked up the phone and dialed his grandmother's number again. This time the phone rang. Bingo straightened and took a deep breath.

The phone rang and rang and rang. Bingo let it ring twenty times before he finally hung up.

Then he moved to the sofa and sat watching out the window for his grandmother.

She's been admitted, he thought.

On Holding Hands

"Hi, Mom."

"Oh, Bingo, come in."

Bingo walked into his mother's hospital room and stood awkwardly by her bed. He said, "Dad will be up in a minute. He had to park the car."

There was a tube in his mother's arm, and a clear liquid was dripping through it. If it wasn't for that and for the unfamiliar hospital gown and for a sort of worried expression in her eyes, she looked perfectly normal.

Bingo said, "How are you?"

"Well, I'm all right for the moment."

"You look fine."

"I am, but I may have to stay in bed for a while."

"How long?"

"I don't know. They won't tell you anything in the hospital, Bingo. They won't answer a single question. The nurses say, 'You'll have to ask the doctor,' and the doctor won't even say that much."

She smoothed the spread and let her hands rest on her stomach.

"Does something hurt?" Bingo asked anxiously.

She shook her head. "No. . . . So, what did you do today?" Bingo could see his mother was making a real effort to be interested.

"Nothing much. I mailed Melissa's present. That was about it."

"What'd you get her?"

"Just some earrings."

Bingo wanted his mother to grin and say, "Not *gypsy* earrings?" in a taunting way. He would willingly allow her to taunt him if it would help her feel more cheerful.

His mother, however, wasn't up to her usual taunts tonight. She smoothed the spread over her stomach again.

Bingo cleared his throat. "Tomorrow I'm going to make your fudge."

"My what?"

"The old-timey fudge, remember? You said that's what you wanted for Christmas."

"Oh, don't bother with that, Bingo."

"I want to make it for you."

"I don't want any fudge."

"Maybe you don't right now, but by Christmas—"

"No, don't bother." She sighed. "All I want is to hold on to this baby."

"Of course."

This was the second time Bingo had visited someone in the hospital, and hospitals made Bingo nervous. He saw so many things he didn't want to have happen to him.

He had been nervous the first time too, but Melissa had been with him then. He and Melissa had held hands.

And, Bingo decided, if you had to visit someone in the hospital, it was definitely a good idea to have someone along to hold your hand.

Bingo remembered how natural that hand-holding had been. He and Melissa were visiting their teacher Mr. Mark who had been in a motorcycle accident.

They were both nervous, but they were trying not to show it. They were walking down the hall, not even thinking about such a thing as holding hands, and then as they entered Mr. Mark's hospital room, they had reached for each other at the exact same moment. It was the nicest, most natural, most unplanned thing in the world, as if their hands couldn't help themselves.

Then later he, like a stupid idiot, had started worrying about how to let go! What a child he had been! He was afraid they would hold hands all the way to the car, of all things, that they would have to get in the car holding hands, that that would be awkward—well, it would have been awkward with Melissa in the front seat and him in the back.

Melissa had been the one to let go. "My hand's getting sweaty," she had said.

Well, if he had Melissa's hand now he wouldn't let go no matter how sweaty it got.

Bingo put his hands in his pockets. He said, "I wonder what's keeping Dad."

A woman in the next bed was watching a movie on the ceiling television, and Bingo glanced up at the screen. He wasn't interested in the movie, but he didn't seem to have anywhere else to look.

Bingo and the woman watched the movie together for a moment. A large quantity of something resembling red jelly was oozing down some steps.

The woman smiled at him. *"The Blob,"* she said.

Bingo said, "Ah." It was a word Bingo never used outside of the doctor's office, and it sounded strange, out of place in a hospital room.

Bingo glanced at the woman out of the side of his eyes. Her stomach was flat so she'd probably had her baby, and she was cheerful so she'd probably gotten what she wanted.

The woman said, "I'm only watching this because I have a thing about Steve McQueen."

His mom said, "Oh, Sam, there you are." Both Bingo and his mother looked at his father in the doorway with real gratitude.

His father crossed the room and took her hand. "How's it going?"

"Oh, fine, but this is terrible. I should be home. The tree is half-trimmed. I haven't made a single cookie. I—"

"Hey, I didn't know you knew how to make cookies," he said in a gently teasing way.

"Well, I call those little rum balls I make cookies. I was going to make those."

"Bingo can whip up some rum balls."

"And, oh, Bingo." She turned her face to him as if she'd just remembered he was there. "Bingo, I was planning to get you a new jacket. Ever since you showed me how short the sleeves were on your old one, I've felt guilty."

"They aren't that short," Bingo said graciously, extending his arms. "And my arms do seem to have stopped growing for the moment." He was glad to have some good news to report.

"Bingo," she said seriously, "will you do something for me?"

"Yes."

"Will you buy yourself a jacket?"

"Yes."

"And wrap it?"

"Yes."

"And put it under the tree?"

His dad said, "Next you'll be asking him to look surprised when he opens it!"

His mother smiled at last. "And, Bingo, listen, you can call Melissa long-distance, if you like."

Bingo gasped with surprise. It was as if his mother had read his mind, as if she had been lying there knowing that he was standing there thinking about holding Melissa's hand. To throw her off the track he raised his eyebrows innocently and said, "Melissa?"

"Yes, Melissa."

"Mom, I think I should warn you that she is still in Oklahoma."

"I know that."

"Mom, you said I could never call her again until I worked off the fifty-five dollars for previous calls. I've got about ten more dollars to go."

"Well, it's Christmas."

Bingo glanced up at the television, even though the thought of calling Melissa long-distance had left him oblivious to the Blob. Once again, it was the only place to look.

Television did serve a useful purpose, Bingo thought. It gave people a place to look when they didn't have any other place to look.

On the screen things were coming to a climax. Soldiers were breaking in the door of the high school.

The woman sensed Bingo's attention and explained quickly, "They have to get fire extinguishers. See, the Blob can't stand cold. Fire extinguishers are full of something called CO_2."

Bingo said, "Ah."

Why was he saying all these *ah*s? Did the *ah*s sound as strange to everyone else as they did to him? Was it a sort of medicinal *ah* or—

Bingo's dad said, "Bingo, why don't you go down to the gift shop and get your mom a magazine."

"Sure, I'd be glad to."

As his dad handed him the money, the woman said, "Later they'll drop the Blob off in Antarctica, wherever that is, but they don't actually show it."

"Maybe that's because they're going to let it slip off on the way, like onto Cincinnati so they can have a sequel." Bingo broke off and told them all, "Well, I'll be right back."

A Wall of Silence

Bingo was sitting by the phone, trying to decide if he wanted to call Melissa now or later. He wanted to call now, of course. However, if he did call now, then he couldn't call later, and Bingo knew he would want to call later too.

While he was thinking about this, he reached out and rested one hand on the phone. The phone startled him by ringing.

Since his hand was already on it, there was nothing Bingo could do but pick it up. "Hello?"

A girl's voice said, "Bingo?"

Bingo's dad called from the bedroom, "Is that your mom? If it is, I want to talk to her."

"No, Dad, it's for me." Into the telephone Bingo said, "This is Bingo."

"Hi, it's me again, Boots."

"Yes—Boots."

Bingo felt he had to say her name because she was probably more sensitive about being named Boots than he was
about being named Bingo. Certainly it could not be pleasant to be named for footwear.

"Bingo, I just wanted to apologize for getting so upset
on the phone the other day."

"You didn't get upset—Boots."

"I did too! I threatened to cry!"

"Well . . ."

"And it was silly. I was just so excited when I saw *Gypsy
Lover* on my sister's bookcase, and then when you said
yours was a different *Gypsy Lover,* well, I just wanted to
cry, well, not cry, but like—"

Bingo's dad called, "Don't tie up the phone, Bingo. Your
mom might be trying to call."

"—like when you're sad, you cry; when you're, like,
disappointed, which is what I was, then you get upset,
which I did."

"Oh, I get upset myself sometimes."

"I know—like in the mall that day. That's what attracted
me to you."

"What?" Bingo said. He thought he hadn't heard right.

"That's what attracted me to you!" she repeated.

Bingo, learning that he had heard exactly right, let out
a sort of cry. His mother would probably have called it a
hoarse cry, Bingo thought, and this time his mother would
have been correct.

Bingo's heart began to sink. Although he was experienced in holding mixed-sex conversations—by this time he

had had over a dozen of them—he was not experienced in ending them. And this was one of those mixed-sex conversations that needed ending.

"That," Boots continued as if he had not cried out—or perhaps she heard hoarse cries so often she placed no importance on them, "and, like, that you're a writer. I love intelligence. I feel so stretched when I'm with an intelligent person."

Bingo was now unable to speak at all. He couldn't even swallow. His heart had moved up into his throat and was stuck there like a cork.

Boots said, "What attracted you to me?"

A silence followed.

The silence lengthened.

Bingo realized that this silence was stretching into one of the longest silences that had ever taken place on telephone lines. And it was fast becoming a silence that could never be broken, Bingo knew that much about silences. Certainly he couldn't break it. And she obviously wouldn't.

He was becoming tied by silence to a girl named, of all things, Boots. And the tie was as binding as if rope was involved.

It was an absolute silence now. Boots wasn't even breathing into the phone.

For a brief moment, Bingo wondered if she had taken the easy way out and fainted, like girls did in olden times. But if she had, wouldn't she have dropped the phone? Wouldn't there have been a clunk and a dial tone?

His mind burned with questions.

Wasn't there some way the telephone company had of dealing with emergency silences like this? Didn't they monitor lines to make sure they were being spoken into? Was there any hope the operator would break in and say, "If you're through using this line, please hang up. If you need assistance in hanging up, please hang up and dial the operator."

No such miracle occurred, however, and the silence continued.

How long could a silence like this go on, Bingo wondered—for eternity? Infinity? Would the *National Enquirer* write it up? BINGO AND BOOTS BOUND BY SILENCE—NOW IN TWENTIETH YEAR?

Bingo closed his eyes in desperation. In darkness, the silence took on shape and form. It was as hard as concrete. It was so unyielding that if he stretched out his hand, he could actually feel it like a wall surrounding—

He broke off. He had heard of this phenomenon! It was a wall of silence! He was entombed in a—

"Bingo!"

Bingo looked up, startled. His eyes were glazed with the horror of his recent entombment. He saw his father dimly, as if through a mist.

"Bingo!"

The mist began to recede. His father's form, his face became distinct. Bingo saw with joy that he could even make out the frown on his father's face.

"Bingo, I asked you not to tie up the phone. Your mother might be trying to call."

Bingo gasped "Thank you" to his father.

These two words, although barely audible, served to release him from the spell of silence. He now felt he was capable of speech.

He spoke into the phone. His voice was as normal as if he had used it only five minutes ago instead of twenty years. "My dad just came into the room. He says I have to hang up now. Good-bye—Boots."

Bingo put down the phone. He stood and faced his father who was still standing in the doorway. His frown had softened to a look of puzzlement.

"Dad—"

"What?"

"Anytime you see me sitting with the phone in my hand—this is really important to me—anytime you see me sitting there and I'm not saying anything and you don't think anybody's saying anything to me, then you say the exact same thing you just said."

"I'll try to remember that, Bingo."

"Because what you said was perfect."

Bingo walked past his father and into his room. He lay down on his bed.

Well, one thing had come out of all this, Bingo thought. A decision had been made. He was incapable of another mixed-sex conversation any time in the immediate future.

He would definitely call Melissa later . . . much later.

The Fifth Floor

"Bingo, when I say who this is, please, please don't hang up. It's Boots."

Bingo did not hang up, but he held the phone away from his ear so it wasn't touching him anymore.

"Yes, Boots?"

"Well, the other day when I called—I'm not talking about the in-between times, like when I called and your dad said you couldn't come to the phone. This call is not about the times you couldn't come to the phone, it's about the other *day* when you did come to the phone. Do you remember?"

In Bingo's mind the silence rose again, as powerful and eternal as the Great Wall of China.

"Yes."

"And remember how I asked you what attracted you to me?"

"Yes."

"Well, what I meant was—I *knew* you weren't attracted to *me,* but, like, I thought you might be attracted to some *part* of me. Like people tell me I have nice hair, so you could have said 'hair,' or something like that, 'legs,'— except that you wouldn't have said 'legs' because you've never seen me out of jeans, have you?"

"Not that I remember."

"Oh. But, anyway, I hope you will accept this as my explanation."

"I will."

"And, Bingo, one more thing."

"Yes?"

"I won't be calling anymore."

"Oh." Out of politeness, Bingo tried not to put all the relief into that *Oh* that he was feeling.

"My sister told my mom that I'd been reading *Gypsy Lover* to a boy over the phone, and so I'm forbidden to call you except to, like, apologize."

"Oh."

"But you can call me. I can take calls, but I can't make them."

"Good-bye—Boots."

Bingo was reliving this phone conversation in his mind as he went up on the elevator to the fifth floor. His spirits seemed to be rising along with his body.

Even an unwelcome conversation could be dealt with manfully. And if a silence did develop in spite of all a man's efforts, then the man could walk with the phone to the front door—Bingo had checked the length of the cord and this was possible—the man could walk with the phone to the front door, press the doorbell—*ding-dong*—and say, "Oh, there's someone at the front door. I must go."

This would not be a lie. There would be someone at the front door. The fact that the someone at the door was the same someone who was on the phone . . . Bingo was getting to the point in life where lies seemed unmanly.

It also seemed to Bingo that people didn't place as much importance on adulthood as they used to. Nobody ever said, "Be a man," or "Be a woman." It was as if becoming an adult was something that just came with age.

Maybe so, but Bingo wasn't going to take any chances with his adulthood. When something felt unmanly, he was not going to do it anymore.

Bingo's thoughts trailed off as he approached his mother's door.

Bingo's mother had now been in the hospital for three days, and Bingo was used to it. He actually enjoyed visiting her now. There was an air of festivity on the fifth floor.

The nurses had put up a little tree, and the babies in the nursery were being stuffed into stockings when they went

home. Bingo enjoyed seeing the little round faces peering seriously, yet hopefully, out of the red flannel stockings. Babies made extremely nice stocking stuffers.

The nurses knew his name by now, and one of the older nurses—a Mrs. Hanna—had come in to say she had been in the delivery room the very night when Bingo popped into the world.

"Really? Then can I ask you something?" he had said. "This is something I've wondered about all my life."

"Ask away."

"The doctor that delivered me—did he say 'Bingo' every time a baby popped out?"

She thought about it. "No, I believe that was the only time he ever did that."

That had made Bingo feel better about his name and about himself.

He entered his mother's room with a smile. His mother had a new roommate who had just had twin girls.

"I was trying so hard not to have them till New Year's Eve," the women was telling Bingo's mother tearfully. "If you have the first baby born in the New Year, see, you get lots of presents. Sky City gives you a complete layette. Rogers' jewelers gives a silver rattle."

"Look, you'll manage," his mother told her.

"I'm not sure I can manage one, much less—!" She held up two fingers for emphasis. Then she pulled a tissue from a holder and blotted first one eye and then the other. "Plus, one of them has a flat nose."

"Oh, no, they're pretty."

"They'd better be because I sure can't afford plastic surgery."

Bingo's mother turned to him with a smile. She rubbed her hands together. "Bingo, where's the fudge?"

"What?"

"Didn't you make the fudge?"

"You told me not to!"

"I said that out of depression. Bingo, you knew I didn't mean it."

"Mom!"

"Bingo, quit kidding and bring out the fudge."

His mother's cheeks were pink and she had a girlish glow. There was something about being on an all-girl floor that seemed to sharpen the femininity of the patients, Bingo thought. And something about being on a floor where babies were being stuffed into decorative stockings and sent out into a world bright with artificial lights brought out their playfulness.

Anyway, Bingo hoped this was playfulness, because he really and truly had not made any fudge.

The woman in the next bed said, "Plus I'm a welfare patient and they're going to kick me and the twins out tomorrow. If I could only have held on to those twins for ten more days . . ." She reached for another tissue.

"I'm trying for three weeks," Bingo's mother said with a smile. She crossed her hands over her stomach and looked up at the ceiling as if into the future.

Then she brought herself back and looked at Bingo.

"Bingo, I keep going over this in my mind. I'm thirty-two weeks pregnant. Full-term is forty weeks, so I've got eight weeks to go.

"Now, for every week that I hold on to this baby, he gains five or six ounces. Now right now he probably weighs four and a half pounds. But in three weeks he would weigh over five pounds.

"I feel like if I can just hang on for three more weeks, we'll have it made."

"Lots of luck," the mother of twins said sourly.

At a Darkened Window

"Good night, Harrison."

"Good night, Grammy. Thanks for the ride."

"You are more than welcome. I'll talk to you tomorrow."

Bingo got out of the car and shut the door. He started up the walkway and then stopped. Bingo had just seen something he didn't like.

At the side of the house, at Bingo's window, there was a menacing figure. The menacing figure was beating his fist on the side of the house.

Behind him, his grandmother's Honda drove away, but Bingo continued to stand in place. He didn't even bother waving at the car as he usually did.

The figure had a familiar menacing look. And the cries from the figure had a familiar menacing sound. "Hey, Worm Brain!"

Bingo straightened his shoulders. He had never seen

Wentworth from this view. He had only seen Wentworth's face, framed in the window.

Seeing it from here, Bingo realized what a serious breach of etiquette, to say nothing of manliness, it was. He was incensed by it. This was one menacing figure that was going to regret menacing.

Bingo started forward. The lights from the Wentworths' Christmas decorations, blinking on and off, lit the way.

Bingo's steps were quick but quiet, and he closed the distance between himself and Wentworth without a sound.

"What are you doing?" he asked. His quiet voice seemed to crackle with just the right mixture of authority and outrage, creating electricity in the still night.

Billy Wentworth swung around. His arms were up, stiffened into dangerous weapons, ready to deliver something, Bingo knew, they had been wanting to deliver for years. His mouth was pulled back in a snarl.

Bingo stood firm, arms at his sides.

"Don't do that!" Wentworth said. "I thought you had better sense than to sneak up on me. Don't ever sneak up on me! That's a good way to get your head chopped off! Man, I've had karate!"

"And breaking into people's windows," Bingo went on, all authority now, "is a good way to get arrested."

"I was knocking on your window, not breaking in, Worm Brain."

"So you say."

They looked at each other. It was Wentworth who began to sag first. "I'm in trouble, Bingo." The use of the name

Bingo rather than the usual Worm Brain told Bingo the
trouble must be serious.

"What'd you do?"

"Remember I asked you if you thought Cici was going
to give me something for Christmas?"

"Yes, and I said I thought she wasn't because she
couldn't stand the sight of you." Not only was Bingo not
going to flinch from a karate chop, he also had no intention
of flinching from the truth.

"Yes, you do remember." Billy Wentworth swallowed.
"But I couldn't get it off my mind. I wanted her to give
me something. I wanted to see what it would be. I never
got anything from a girl before."

Bingo was glad he was not in that bleak position. He
had gotten many, many—well, actually he had only gotten
one, but it was the kind of extraordinary gift that left him
with the feeling that girls had been showering him with
gifts for years.

"So then I thought, what's stopping *you*," he pointed to
himself, "that's me, from giving *her* something." He
pointed to an imaginary Cici. "Then *she*," another point
at Cici, "will have to give *me* something back."

There was a pause. Bingo said, "So?" even though he
really didn't want to hear any more.

"So, I said to my mom, 'I've got to give this girl a Christmas present and I don't have anything to give. She said,
'Get something out of the reject drawer.' See, my mom has
a whole drawer full of things she has gotten that she didn't
want, notepaper and decorated soaps, things like that—

this is where we do our shopping for teachers. My sister got a nice scarf for Miss Prunty, her music teacher, just last week."

Billy Wentworth swallowed. Bingo waited.

"I go to the drawer and open it. Pickings are slim because everybody's been at it, it being Christmas, but there was one decent bottle of perfume. I know Cici uses perfume because I've smelled it on her."

"I've smelled it too."

"I go back in the kitchen. I say, 'Mom, how about this bottle of perfume?' My mom doesn't look up—she's putting Decorettes on a cake in a Christmas tree design—but she knows the bottle of perfume and nods. She goes, 'Fine, but don't take the after-shave. I'm saving that for the postman.'"

"I said, 'I would hardly give a girl after-shave.' Bingo, I was insulted."

"Of course."

"So, I go in—Mom keeps the wrapping paper and stuff on a card table in her bedroom and I wrap up the perfume and get a gift tag. I'm in such a hurry that I just initial the tag. 'To: C. C. From: B. W.' Like that."

"Which said it all." Bingo was tired and he wished he could go in the house and listen to the rest of this from a chair at the window, like a priest at confession, but he continued to stand where he was.

"And then I delivered it—Bingo, I couldn't wait. I had to deliver it then and there. I don't know why—something came over me. It was an—an urge."

Bingo felt a twinge of sympathy at that. He was all too familiar with urges.

"I delivered it on my bike. Cici wasn't there, so I delivered it to her mother. I rode home. I put my bike in the garage. I went in the house—" He was reciting the story now, as if he were on the witness stand and had to get every detail correct.

"My mom was rooting through the reject drawer, saying, 'I know I had a bottle of after-shave—I know I had a bottle of after-shave—'

"Bingo, my blood turned to ice water—you know how it does in books? Like a soldier will be sitting there, thinking he is safe and suddenly he hears a faint click behind him, and he knows that someone just clicked off the safety on his semiautomatic? And his blood turns to ice water? You know that feeling?"

"Sort of."

"Well, my blood turned to ice water because I knew I had given Cici the postman's after-shave."

There was a long pause. The Wentworths' Christmas lights blinked on and off. In the on-off glow of the Christmas lights, Wentworth's face seemed to be throbbing with pain.

Finally Bingo said, "These things happen, Wentworth."

"I haven't told you the worst."

"There's more?"

"It wasn't just plain after-shave. It was Brut! I gave Cici Boles Brut!"

In his agony he turned his back on Bingo entirely.

"Look," Bingo said, "well, listen. Go buy Cici a real present. Spend some money. Earrings. That's what I got Melissa. I'll lend you the fifty-nine cents. Take the earrings over and say, 'Mrs. Boles, when I delivered Cici's present, I got it mixed up. Here is Cici's real present and may I please have the postman's after-shave.' She'll give it to you."

Wentworth was shaking his head.

"She will."

More head-shaking.

"Come on. She's a mother. She'll have to."

Wentworth said, "No."

Then he turned and looked directly into Bingo's eyes. A gorilla had once done this to Bingo at the zoo, leaving Bingo unsettled for hours. Only the gorilla had had a sort of human, intelligent look, while Wentworth's eyes were those of a wounded animal.

"But you, Bingo," he said in a pleading voice that didn't go with the gorilla eyes. "She would give it to you."

Midnight Tonight and Brut by Tomorrow

"Listen, Worm Brain, I want that Brut by tomorrow—or else!"

"But it's m-midnight. I can't go over to the Boles's at m-midnight."

"You are not getting the message, Mush Mouth. I *want* the Brut."

"I'll honestly try, but—"

"You better honestly try, because if I don't get the Brut—"

"You will—"

"Don't interrupt. You know I don't like to be interrupted. If I don't get that Brut by tomorrow morning, then you'll get one of these—" *Zoink!* "Followed by one of these—" *Pow!* "And a few of these—" *Zap-a-zap zap zap!*

Silence.

"And, remember, there's plenty more where they came from. Now get up off the ground. Get up! What? You say you can't get up? Then I've got a way of getting you up—up and into orbit."

Bingo groaned.

"Get up, son," another voice said.

Now two people were demanding that he get up. Didn't they think he wanted to get up? But how many *Zoinks* and *Pows* and *Zap-a-zap zap zaps* could a body take?

"Bingo, wake up!"

"What?"

"Wake up, son."

"Oh, Dad. Dad?"

"Yes. Bingo—"

"Oh, thanks, Dad, thanks. I was having a terrible nightmare. See, Wentworth was trying to get me to go over and get the postman's after-shave from Cici Boles, and he lost patience—well, actually, he did much, much more than lose patience. This was more like losing control. He socked me here and here and four real quick jabs—"

"I haven't got time to listen to that now, son. They've just taken your mom to the delivery room, and I'm going to the hospital to be with her."

"What?"

"Get on some clothes, Bingo. I'm dropping you off at Grammy's."

"What happened?"

Bingo's dad pulled back the covers and helped Bingo to his feet. "I'll tell you on the way. Get dressed."

"What time is it?"

"Midnight."

"But I saw Mom just—like five hours ago and she was fine. She wanted fudge!"

Bingo's dad handed him his jeans, and Bingo pulled them on over his pajamas. His dad helped him into his jacket and zipped it up.

The overhead light seemed unusually bright—it always did at midnight, and Bingo shielded his eyes with one hand.

"Shoes, son, where are your shoes?"

Bingo knelt and pulled them out from under the bed. He didn't bother with socks, and the insides of his shoes were cold and gritty.

"Grammy will bring you back in the morning for whatever you need. Let's go!"

Bingo ran after his father. "But, Dad, listen, Mom was saying that if she could just hold on for three more weeks the baby would weigh over five pounds."

"Well, she couldn't . . ."

Bingo had to pause to retrieve a shoe—he hadn't had time to lace them up so they wouldn't stay on—and when he got to the garage, his father was already in the car with the motor running.

Bingo slid in beside him. "So, what happened?"

"I didn't get all the details. She started having pains about an hour ago."

"But she had pains before and they stopped."

"This time her water broke—that's the bag that the baby's in. Once it breaks, they want mothers to deliver within twenty-four hours."

His father went around a corner too fast, and the wheels

of the station wagon squealed in protest. Bingo reached for his seat belt and clicked it into place.

He glanced at his father. He said, "Seat belt, Dad." His parents, like an endangered species, were taking on new value.

His father fastened his seat belt without slowing down. His profile was sharper than Bingo remembered, maybe because his mouth was set in a straight line that was unfamiliar to Bingo.

"So, go on about Mom."

"Where was I?"

"The bag had just broken."

"When that happens, the barrier between the baby and the outside world is gone and is open to infection."

Bingo slumped in his seat. He felt as if the same thing had happened to him, as if the barrier between him and the outside world was gone and he was open to anything.

"How long is this going to take?" he asked.

"Well, you took eight hours."

"So sometime between eight hours and twenty-four hours we ought to know something."

"We ought to."

The car pulled up in front of his grandmother's condo. She must have been watching for them, because she opened the door immediately and stepped out under the porch light.

Bingo turned to his father. "Call me, Dad."

"I will."

"Don't forget."

"I won't."

"Dad—"

"I'm in a hurry, Bingo. What is it?"

"Oh, nothing."

Bingo got out of the car.

"Give her my love!" his grandmother called, waving from the porch.

Bingo's dad waved back and drove off in the direction of the hospital.

With his shoes flapping forlornly, Bingo started up the walk.

BO from the Coop

Bingo was drinking his first cup of coffee—ever. After the first bitter sip he had thought he would not be able to get the whole thing down, but now he was beginning to like it.

It wasn't that he liked the taste—no one could like that. What he liked was the feeling of companionship that came over two adults when they sat drinking a basically bad-tasting liquid together. The two adults were Bingo and his grandmother.

Bingo's grandmother had just about spoiled the companionship by telling him, "Actually, Bingo, this isn't real coffee."

"No? Then what is it?"

"Sanka."

"Does real coffee taste any better?"

She smiled at him over the rim of her cup. "One tastes

just about as bad as the other. You ought to put some milk and sugar in it."

"That would be childish."

Bingo put down his mug, but he kept his hands around it for the warmth.

He said, "You know, Grammy, I was feeling very successful yesterday evening. That's what a good day does for me."

He lifted his mug with both hands and looked at her through the steam. "You want to hear all the good things about yesterday?"

"I would love to hear some good things about yesterday."

He put down his cup so he could count off the triumphs. "Well, first, I acted quite manly on the telephone—see, this girl called me that I didn't want to talk to and she had called me before, which was how I knew I didn't want to talk to her, but I did talk to her and very politely." He broke off to say, "Look, maybe I won't go into each one in detail, I'll just list them, all right?"

"All right, but we have plenty of time."

"Yeah, I guess so. Well. One—I acted manly on the phone. Two—I had a nice visit with Mom, and she was hopeful about the baby. Three—I went out to eat with you and I didn't spill anything. Four—I caught this big boy looking in my window and when I went up to him, I startled him and he turned around with his arms up like this in a karate stance, and I did not flinch."

Bingo looked deep into his Sanka. "That may not sound

like much of a day to you, Grammy, but for me, well, it was practically the highlight of December."

"I think it sounds like a fine day."

He sighed. "And then . . ."

"Then what?"

"This! Mom! The baby! The baby is coming and it doesn't weigh enough!"

"We don't know that."

"Well, I know it. Mom said four pounds, and four pounds isn't enough."

"Four and a half pounds."

"Well, all right, but have you ever seen four and a half pounds of hamburger? It's—"

"It might not have been enough in the old days, but today they have special care for premature infants. They can work miracles." His grandmother paused before she continued. "You know what I was thinking about while I was waiting for Sam to drop you off?"

"What?"

"I was remembering the night you were born."

Bingo stopped and waited. Although he wasn't through expressing his concern over the baby's weight, he found this new topic appealing. Bingo enjoyed hearing his grandmother tell stories in which he had played an important part.

He couldn't resist. "What was so special about the night I was born?"

"Oh, it was a beautiful night—full moon. It was so bright you could see the mountains.

"Your mom had told me, 'Now I'm not going to call when we go to the hospital because I don't want you to worry.' But I kept after her and kept after her. I said, 'I want to worry. It's the kind of thing I like to worry about.' So finally she said, 'Well, when we drive by your condo'—which was right on the way to the hospital—'When we drive by your condo, I'll give you a honk. When you hear the Coop, you can start worrying.' "

"The Coop?"

"At that time your mom and dad were still driving a car we'd gotten your mom in college. It was an old Chevy and your mom called it the Coop. 'I'll pick you up in the Coop,' she'd tell her friends. One summer she took seventeen girls to the lake in the Coop.

"Anyway, Bingo, the Coop had a very distinctive horn. It was like a foghorn. This was before your time, Bingo, but there used to be an old commercial for deodorant, and a voice would go, 'B—O.' The O was lower. 'B—O.' Like that. Back then BO stood for body odor."

"It still does."

"So in the middle of the night, I heard the Coop's horn go 'B—O.' And I knew you were on your way into the world."

"Grammy, you never told me that before."

"I was saving it." She eyed him. "Bingo, aren't you getting sleepy? Don't you want to lie down for a while?"

"No."

"It's going to be morning before we have any news."

He shook his head.

"Want me to heat up your Sanka?"

Bingo hesitated only a moment. "Please."

When his grandmother put the steaming mug before him, he wrapped his hands around it again. He liked the warmth of it better than the taste.

"Go on about the night I was born."

"Well, I rushed to the window, but the Coop was already out of sight. So I woke up your grandfather and said, 'James, did you hear the Coop?' Because I thought I might have dreamed it, I wanted you to be born so much. He said, 'Yes, I heard the Coop and so did everybody else on the block who was trying to sleep. Now get back in bed.' That was just the way your grandfather talked. He was as excited as I was.

"So, I got back in, but I . . ."

They were still talking about the night Bingo was born when the phone rang.

The Perfect Ten

Bingo's grandmother had a wonderfully hopeful way of answering the phone. "Hell-o!" She sort of sang out the word, as if she knew in advance someone was calling that she really wanted to talk to.

This time, however, she said, "Sam?" It was a hopeful "Sam," but it was anxious too.

Bingo stood up. He and his grandmother were looking straight at each other while she listened. Then she shook her head. She mouthed the words, "Not yet."

Bingo lowered himself back down into his chair.

His grandmother listened and said, "Well, keep us informed." She listened again. "And give her our love."

His grandmother came back to the table. "Your dad says that things are progressing, but slowly. Your mother asked him to call so we wouldn't worry."

"I'm still worried."

"I am too. But your dad's in the delivery room with her. They used to not allow that—they made the dads look through a little round window on the door and they couldn't see anything."

A silence fell over them. It had been possible to divert themselves with Bingo's birth for a while, but not even that interested Bingo now.

Dawn was breaking, and somehow he had expected the baby to be here by now. The only thing he really knew about babies was that they were always born at night—at least everybody he knew had been. It was a nighttime activity.

The realization that dawn was now breaking, that the stupid sun which had never waited for anyone or anything in its whole life, was poking its stupid head—

Tears came to Bingo's eyes and he quickly rubbed them away.

"Bingo, why don't you stretch out on the sofa."

"I don't want to miss anything."

"What could you miss? Sitting at the table with an old woman!"

"Where's the old woman?" Bingo asked gallantly. This was a standing joke between them. "I don't see any old woman."

This caused them both to smile and Bingo said, "All right, I'll lie down if you promise, *promise* you'll wake me when the phone rings. Even before you answer, you have to wake me."

"I promise."

Bingo went in the living room and lay down on the sofa. His grandmother covered him with an afghan she had crocheted using sixteen different colors of yarn.

"Remember, you promised to wake me."

"Yes."

Bingo closed his eyes, and fell immediately into a deep sleep. It was such a deep sleep that when he awakened, four hours later, he was still lying on his back, still covered by the afghan, arms still at his sides.

The only thing different was that the taste of Sanka in his mouth had strengthened or soured or done something to make his entire mouth taste—he searched for the right word—fetid.

Bingo was always pleased with the use of a new word, particularly when no other word would do. Sanka left a mouth fetid. Enough said.

Bingo could hear his grandmother doing something in the kitchen, and he came to his senses. He remembered what he was doing in this condo, on this sofa, under this afghan.

He threw off the afghan and went to the door. "You didn't wake me!"

"Bingo, there was nothing to wake you for."

"Dad hasn't called yet?"

"No."

"But it's—" He looked at his watch. "It's after ten o'clock!"

"I know. Want some Sanka?"

"No, I've sworn off that stuff." Bingo slumped into a chair.

"Well, how about some bacon and eggs or some cereal?"

"Not right now. I'm not awake yet."

He combed his hair with his hands and left his fingers in the tangles. He looked up.

"Grammy, do you remember how I acted when I first found out about the baby?"

"Well, yes. . . ."

"All I thought about was how a baby would upset my life, *my* life."

"Well, it was a shock to you, Bingo."

"And now I realize that, well, it would have upset my life, but there's such a thing as a welcome upset. And now I realize that's what a baby brother would have been—a very pleasant upset, one that would have added to my life."

He ducked his head.

"And now all I can think about is how much it's going to upset my life if the baby brother doesn't—" He paused for the right word. "—doesn't happen."

"It's going to happen. It's going to happen."

They looked at each other across the sunlit kitchen. "And while we're waiting for it to happen," his grandmother added, "I'm going to fix us some breakfast."

She opened the cabinet where she kept her pots and pans and pulled out a small skillet. At that moment the phone rang, and Grammy picked it up on the first ring.

"Sam?" She listened. "Oh, Sam."

She put the skillet over her heart and turned to Bingo. Tears filled her eyes. "He's here," she told Bingo. "Jamie's here. They're both all right."

She put down the skillet and held out the phone to Bingo. "You talk to your dad. I've got to lie down. Look, I'm starting to shake."

"Dad?"

"Bingo! Jamie was born fifteen minutes ago."

"Is he all right?"

"He and your mom are fine."

"How big is he?"

"Well, he's small—four pounds, fifteen ounces, but he gave a loud cry in the delivery room. I can't tell you how good that sounded to me. He got a score of two on his cry—that's as good as a baby can get."

"He got scores?"

"Every baby born in the United States does. It's called an Apgar score."

"And two is good?"

"It's the best. They checked him at one minute, and his score was eight—out of a possible ten. He got a two on his respiratory effort—that's his cry, a two on his heart rate, a one on his color—"

"What was wrong with his color?"

"Well, his body was pink, but his extremities—his arms and legs—were blue. He got a two on his reflex irritability and a one on his muscle tone. Then—"

"What was wrong with his muscle tone?"

"He didn't kick as well as they wanted him to."

"Well, he couldn't! His legs were blue!"

"Then they scored him again at five minutes—that's the most important score. At five minutes, his color was good and so was his kick. He got all twos. Bingo, your baby brother is a perfect ten!"

The Stocking Stuffers

"It's hard for me to believe it's Christmas eve."

"Not for me, Bingo, I feel very Christmasy," his grandmother answered.

They were in his grandmother's Honda, driving to the hospital. Bingo had on his favorite jeans, his favorite shirt, and his favorite jacket—his new one.

He would have to give his mother an explanation for that, of course. His explanation would be, "Mom, you told me to wrap it up and put it under the tree and I did those things. You didn't tell me I had to wait till Christmas to wear it, so I didn't."

He knew his mother wouldn't care. She would understand that he wanted to look especially nice today.

He flipped down the sun visor and checked his image in the mirror underneath.

"You look fine," his grandmother said.

"You do too."

"I was saving this pants suit for something special, and I said to myself, well, there's never going to be anything more special than this, that's for sure, and so I put it on. Then I had bought this purse for myself for Christmas— ever since I was a little girl, Bingo, I have always given myself a Christmas present. The family used to laugh about it. 'To Rose, From Rose,' the cards used to say. This is what I got myself this year."

They drove in silence for a few blocks, and then his grandmother said, "One thing, Bingo . . ."

"What?"

"Don't expect too much."

"What do you mean by that?"

"Well, just that sometimes new babies— Oh, sometimes they're wrinkled, and maybe a little discolored—"

"Dad said he got a two on his color. Dad says he's a perfect ten!"

"I know, but sometimes— Oh, the face is puffy or— When your mom was born, one of her ears was lying flat on her cheek, like that." She pressed her own ear forward.

"Grammy, I've been looking in the nursery every day since Mom was admitted. I know what newborn babies look like."

"Yes, but every baby you've seen has been full-term."

"Sure, but full-term doesn't mean beautiful. I've seen some pointed heads and flat noses. I'm not blind. I've seen hair sticking up like a punk rocker's. But with all that, I never saw one that was really and truly what you would call ugly."

"That's what I wanted to hear."

His grandmother parked the car and they walked together into the hospital.

As they rode to the fifth floor, Bingo said, "If someone had told me last Christmas that I would be doing this this Christmas, well, I . . ."

The door to the fifth floor opened and Bingo stepped out. All morning long Bingo had had an urge to get to the nursery. And now, as he started down the corridor, the urge grew into a need and then into a frenzy. He broke into a run.

Behind him his grandmother called, "Wait for me."

But he couldn't wait. He couldn't be stopped. He was like Roadrunner, with his legs moving so swiftly they were an invisible blur to all the considerate people who were stepping aside to let him pass.

He ended up at the nursery window, slightly out of breath. He put one hand on the wall to support himself.

Then he saw his brother.

Bingo would have known him anywhere.

He was the little one in the back.

His grandmother arrived then. "Can you pick him out?"

"He's the little one in the back."

"Oh, he's so tiny!" His grandmother tapped on the window as if to get his attention. "And, Bingo, he favors you!"

"Really?"

"Yes."

"Grammy, why isn't he moving?"

"He's sleeping."

"It doesn't look like—sleep. Anyway, Dad said he was kicking and crying."

"For the first hour after birth, he probably was. Babies are alert when they're first born, watchful, I guess you'd say, and then they fall into a deep sleep."

"For how long?"

"Three or four hours."

His grandmother signaled again, and Bingo realized she was after the nurse's attention, not the baby's. The nurse was getting a baby ready to go home, putting him in his stocking. The baby was awake and seemed to actually enjoy being a stocking stuffer.

When the nurse finished, she looked up and saw them at the window. Bingo's grandmother pointed at the crib in the back. The nurse smiled, nodded, and pushed the crib closer to the window.

"Oh, look at him. Look! Here's Grammy," she said. "Here's your Grammy. Oh, isn't he precious, Bingo? Jamie, here's Grammy. Welcome to the world."

Jamie was all the things his grandmother had warned him about—puffy, discolored, wrinkled, but she hadn't warned him Jamie would have a tube in him.

"What's the tube for?" he asked.

He watched the clear liquid dripping into his brother.

"They're feeding him through that. When a baby's little like Jamie, they cut the cord long in the delivery room so they can feed him through it."

"Oh."

"You know why they wrap them up so tightly in their little blankets?"

"No."

"So they'll feel secure. That's way back from the Bible—swaddling clothes. And you know why they have those little happy faces stuck on each crib? I was so curious I asked about this."

"Why?"

"Because they have learned that little babies, even tiny little babies, can recognize a face. They actually did an experiment on this somewhere. They put up faces on one side of the crib and another design on the other and the babies all watched the faces."

Bingo was finding out so much about babies that he could hardly take it in. These little things had minds! They knew stuff! They—

His grandmother sighed with pleasure, breaking Bingo's train of thought. "I could stand here all day," she said, "couldn't you, Bingo?"

Bingo intended to.

"It's all a miracle to me. This is a room full of miracles," she said.

Then she shifted her Christmas purse and said, "But I do want to run in and see your mother. Are you coming?"

"In a minute."

"Bye-bye, Jamie. Grammy's leaving now. Bye-bye, love, bye-bye, you precious thing."

She left and Bingo drew closer to the window. He wanted to welcome his brother in private.

After the After-Shave

The doorbell rang. Bingo thought it might be the postman with another package.

So he took the fudge off the stove, wiped his hands on his apron, and then proceeded to the door.

As Bingo entered the living room, he could see through the window that it was not the postman. It was Cici Boles. His heart sank, for Cici Boles had a present in one hand.

Bingo continued to the door, but not quite as briskly as before.

"Oh, hello, Cici."

Although he had only opened the door a crack, she managed to slip through the crack and into the living room.

"Bingo, will you do me a favor?" she asked in a rush.

Although Bingo had already wiped his hands on his apron back in the kitchen, he began to do it again. "If—if I can."

Bingo had backed up, and he could now see out of the window. A strange car was parked in front of their house on the wrong side of the street. A strange woman was looking out the car window, watching the house as sharply as if she were a private detective.

The woman was Cici Boles's mother, Bingo thought, and this brought Bingo the first comforting thought of the afternoon. If Mrs. Boles hated to wait in the car for Cici as much as his mother hated to wait in the car for him, then the visit was going to be a short one. *His* mother would have already started sounding the horn.

"The creep next door—" Cici nodded toward the Wentworth house. "That stupid nerd brought this over and left it at my house."

She showed Bingo a poorly wrapped box. He could read the initials on the gift tag—C. C. and B. W.—which Wentworth had printed with such hasty hope.

For a moment Bingo hesitated, wondering if he should launch directly into the story of the reject drawer and Wentworth's shopping spree there.

But the package, while poorly wrapped, did not appear to have been unwrapped. And if it hadn't been unwrapped, then it couldn't have been seen. Cici's anger was, therefore, about something other than receiving Brut.

Bingo decided to maintain silence, but his hands began to twitch with eagerness. The postman's Brut was within his grasp. If he kept his cool . . .

"That *nerd* had the nerve to bring me *this*."

"Er, what is it?"

"I don't know! Some stupid stuff! You can smell it through the paper."

She thrust the package under Bingo's nose. Bingo inhaled the faint, pleasant scent of Brut.

"Possibly perfume," he said tactfully.

He raised one hand to take it, but she had already pulled it away. She lifted it to her own nostrils. "It doesn't smell like any perfume I ever smelled before."

Bingo extended his hand as if to have another smell. "May I?"

"I stormed around the house and stormed around the house." The package went with her as she stormed around Bingo's living room, recreating the scene. "So finally my mom goes, 'Well, you don't have to accept the thing, you know. You can always refuse it. Give it back.'

"I said, 'I can?' Because I didn't know that, did you, Bingo?"

"I did read that—I believe it was in 'Dear Abby,' and you can usually trust her."

His hands were twitching so hard now he had to put them in his apron pockets.

"But you have to do it *before* you open the package, my mom says, or else whoever gave it to you will think that you didn't like the *gift*. My mom was very clear about that. 'You have to make it clear that *no* gift would have been acceptable, otherwise the boy—'

" '—the *nerd*,' I put in.

" 'Otherwise the *boy* might try to get you something else.' "

"Your mother sounds like a sensible woman."

Bingo glanced out the window to see if the sensible woman had, by some miracle, put her hand on the horn. To his dismay, he saw she had turned her attention to the Wentworth house. She was now watching it as closely as if she were trying to see through the siding.

"Well, anyway, that's where you come in."

"Me?"

"Yes, I want you to give it back for me."

Bingo stepped forward. "Why, I'd be glad to."

"You would?"

"Yes."

"I didn't think you'd agree."

"Well, it's Christmas."

"And will you say, 'Cici can't accept this. She's sorry. Her mom doesn't allow her to accept gifts from boys'?"

"Yes."

"Let me hear you."

"Cici can't accept this. She's sorry. Her mom doesn't allow her to accept gifts from boys."

"Oh, Bingo. I'm so glad I came to your house instead of his. I told my mom this was the nerd's house."

"*I'm* the nerd?"

"That's why I came in the house so quickly. My mom has seen him, and if she saw you, she'd know you weren't the nerd."

Outside the horn sounded twice—music to Bingo's ears. He extended his hand.

"I just couldn't face him," Cici said, trying to look pretty and—in Bingo's opinion—failing miserably.

"Of course not. I'll face him for you. I face him all the time. Facing him is nothing to me."

His hand had been extended so long, his muscles were beginning to tire.

"Well . . ."

He reached out and gave the package a gentle tug. Cici did not release it.

"Why are you so eager to have this package?" she asked. She wasn't even trying to look pretty now. Her eyes were narrow with suspicion.

"I'm not so eager."

"You are too!"

"Look, you asked me to give the package back. I said I'd give the package back. If you don't want me to give the package back . . ." He tried to keep the yearning out of his voice, the twitch from his fingers.

"What's in this package, anyway?" Cici asked. She shook the package and Brut sloshed around in the bottle.

"P-perfume, we said, didn't we?"

Cici broke the tape that sealed one end and lifted the flap.

"Don't do that!" Bingo cried.

"Why not?"

"Because if you open it, you can't give it back! Your mother said that and Dear Abby did too."

A low, deliberately handsome voice spoke from the doorway. "What did Dear Abby say?"

Bingo and Cici turned. They stared, openmouthed, at

Billy Wentworth in the doorway. He was smiling, but it was the anxious smile of someone who has recently given after-shave to the girl he loves.

There was a silence. Outside, Cici's mother blew the car horn four times, then four more.

Cici said, "Oh, here!" She rushed at Wentworth and thrust the package into his stomach. "Take that!" He looked as stunned as if she had given him a knockout punch instead of a bottle of after-shave.

She flounced to the door. Then she turned and her face was terrible to behold. Some people should never, ever get angry, Bingo realized, because their faces aren't made for it. If they have little eyes, the eyes get littler. If they have a big nose, it gets bigger. Cici Boles was now a caricature of herself.

Bingo and Billy Wentworth drew together in a sort of unconscious effort at protection.

"And I never want to see either one of you stupid nerds again!"

She ran out the door, down the steps, down the sidewalk, around the car, got in, slammed the door, and said something short to her mother.

"Scratch off!" came immediately to Bingo's mind, for the car shot away from the curb and drove at an accelerated speed out of sight.

Well, never seeing her again wouldn't be any hardship on Bingo, that was for sure, but he was aware he was not the only stupid nerd involved here. The stinging remark had been hurled at dual stupid nerds.

He glanced at the other one.

It was not a pretty sight to watch a man's dreams wither and fall at his feet like autumn leaves, but Bingo did not look away.

"Well," Wentworth said. He squared his shoulders with such manliness that Bingo was proud to live next door to him. "At least I got the postman's after-shave back."

"Yes, that's what counts."

Bingo accompanied him to the porch and stood with his hands in his apron pockets, seeing Wentworth home.

At the Window

Bingo thought the baby was dead. Actually he was sure of it.

Jamie had not moved in fifteen minutes. That was how long Bingo had been standing at the nursery window, and in all that time Jamie had not taken one single breath.

Other babies had howled, yawned, stretched, scrunched up their foreheads, and taken little peeks at the world. One even had the hiccups.

Jamie had done nothing. He did not move, he did not breathe. There could only be one reason for stillness of this nature.

Bingo looked to the nurse for assistance. The nurse was changing another baby—a baby that probably didn't need changing, while his brother who did need attention desperately lay—

The nurse finished changing the baby and glanced up at the window. Bingo hated to ask her to please check and make sure his brother was still alive, because he had already done this several times in the past two days.

She gave him a wry look, went over, and checked Jamie. Then she gave Bingo a smile and an OK signal, and to Bingo's intense relief, Jamie stretched.

Bingo shrugged and smiled back.

Then he went to his mother's room. He always had to check the nursery first thing and last thing, also a few times in between, just to make sure his brother was still breathing.

Bingo's mother said, "Bingo," when he came in the door. It was the way the word is said at bingo parlors when an important game has just been won.

"Hi, Mom."

"Guess what Jamie did this morning," his mother said. "Held my hand."

"Oh, Mom."

"Well, my finger, if you want me to be precise. See, Bingo, you put your finger in his hand—you can try it Friday when we get home—you put your finger in his hand, and his fingers close around it. It's an absolutely incredible feeling. I had forgotten how it was. You used to have little hands like that and—"

She broke off, smiling at herself. "I'm getting as bad as mother." She smoothed her covers over her flat stomach. "Speaking of hands, I hope that is fudge in yours."

"Oh, yes, it is."

Bingo presented the tin and his mother worked off the lid. She inhaled the aroma.

"Oh, Bingo, you used real butter."

"You told me I had to."

"Yes, but I didn't think you'd remember. As I was opening the box I was sort of steeling myself for the aroma of margarine, but it's butter!"

She inhaled again. "This fudge is exactly the way I wanted it to be. Thank you, Bingo."

"You're welcome."

She looked over the pieces and selected one. She put it in her mouth and closed her eyes.

Bingo stood in silence for the verdict. The fudge lasted a long time, but Bingo waited it out.

"Oh, that was wonderful," his mother said finally. "Absolutely wonderful. Pass it to Thelma. Thelma, I want you to have a piece of this wonderful fudge my son made."

Thelma was his mother's new roommate. She had had an eight-pound girl, but Bingo thought she looked as if she might have another one at any minute.

When Bingo first came in the room, Thelma had been combing her hair, watching herself in the mirror that popped up out of her hospital table. As soon as the aroma of fudge filled the room, however, Thelma started watching them.

Dutifully, Bingo crossed to the next bed.

Thelma said, "I can't resist. I'm going on a diet when I get home. Oh, I love fudge." She leaned around Bingo to ask his mother, "How many pieces can I have?"

"As many as you want," Bingo's mother said graciously. Bingo appreciated how hard it must have been for her to be gracious when fudge like this was involved.

"Well, I could eat the whole box, but I'll just take four—no, five."

Thelma snapped down her mirror. She lined the five pieces up on her table like a little train. After a brief deliberation, she ate the caboose.

Bingo's mother took one more piece of fudge before she closed the box. "So, I know that you gave me fudge, and I know you gave Melissa earrings, and I know you gave Jamie a teddy bear."

"That's what everybody gave him," Bingo said. "He's got a teddy bear collection."

"A baby can never have too many teddy bears. But, Bingo, I never heard what you gave your dad."

"A gadget for his desk. He said he liked it. It holds pencils, stamps, paper clips, erasers, rulers, everything. He's already using it."

"Oh, by the by, Bingo, there's one other little matter I've been curious about. Did you ever call Melissa?"

"Not yet. I'm going to do it this afternoon, as soon as I get home."

The Call

"Melissa?"

"Yes."

"It's Bingo."

"Bingo!"

"Yes."

"Oh, Bingo."

There was a silence, but it was a warm, promising silence, a silence warmed with emotion, and promising because Bingo knew what she was thinking and she knew what he was thinking, and they were both thinking the same thing.

Bingo enjoyed a silence like this. It could go on forever, as far as he was conerned.

Melissa said, "I love my earrings."

"Oh, they were just—earrings."

"I've got them on now."

"Really? I wish I could see that."

"Do you like your notebook holder?"

"I love it."

"You aren't just saying that?"

"No, no, I love it. I've got my notebooks in it. I'm starting a new notebook. It's for my brother—just little things, like how I felt when I first saw him and—"

"Bingo! You have a baby brother?"

"Yes, didn't you know?" To Bingo, it was the kind of world-shaking news that reaches everyone instantly, even in remote places like Bixby.

"Oh, Bingo, you're going to make a wonderful big brother."

"I'm going to try," he said. "It's something I really want to succeed at."

"You will!"

"Actually I don't feel exactly like a brother—I feel like, oh, I don't know, like a very, very young grandfather."

"Bingo, listen, I want a picture of the two of you."

"Sure. I can't have it taken yet because the nurses won't let me behind the glass, but Jamie's coming home at the end of the week. He won't weigh quite five pounds, but when the mother is very responsible—which my mom is— they'll sometimes let the baby go home anyway."

It was amazing, Bingo thought, how in the midst of a conversation with Melissa he sometimes forgot it was a mixed-sex conversation. It just seemed so natural for them to be talking. . . .

"I want your faces in the picture, Bingo, so I can tell if you look alike."

"Everyone says we do, except he doesn't have freckles yet, of course."

"He'll get them. And when he does, I want another picture."

"All right."

"This has been a wonderful Christmas for me, Bingo."

"Has it?"

"Yes, and last Christmas was just terrible. My dad was unemployed and we didn't get anything that hadn't been on sale. You know how things that have been on sale have a certain look to them?"

Bingo had been lying on his parents' bed with both their pillows behind his head, relaxing. Now he sat up.

"What kind of look?"

Bingo found that this extremely unwelcome bit of news had activated his alarm system. He had an alarm system that was easily activated and could send panic to every part of his body within seconds, so he made an effort to control the panic. Hopefully, he could put it on hold.

"Oh, just a look. You can always tell."

"How?"

His voice was remarkable for its control. At least he had prevented the panic from reaching—and tightening—his vocal cords.

"How could I explain it? Oh, items that have been on sale have an unwanted look."

In order to keep his alarm system on hold, he decided to analyze this serious accusation.

He brought back to mind the sales table at K Mart. He

remembered every item—every snarled strand of beads, every tarnished ring, every faded bracelet, and he had to admit that they had an unwanted look.

Then he remembered the earrings—the golden earrings. And he found—especially now that he saw them in Melissa's ears—that the remark in no way pertained to the earrings. It was almost, he thought, expanding on the idea, as if the hand of fate had put those earrings on the sales table instead of a clerk in a brown smock.

Melissa was saying, "For example, the only thing my little brother wanted last Christmas was a Ninja Turtle. Did he get it? No. Why not? Because they weren't on sale! And how much does a Ninja Turtle cost?"

Bingo knew she would answer her own question so he glanced at the kitchen timer. He had brought it with him into his parents' room, and it had been ticking away steadily since the first "hello."

Bingo's mother had told him he could talk exactly five minutes—no more, no less—and he did not want the time to get away from him. It had a way of doing that when he talked to Melissa.

"When you hear a loud buzzing sound," he warned her,

"our five minutes will be up. We'll have to say good-bye."

"All right. But, listen, Bingo, I didn't think you were allowed to call me and so, you know what? My grandmother gave me five dollars for Christmas and I was going to use part of it to call you."

"You still can. Or you could just buy a stamp and write me. Your letters—"

The buzzer sounded. Bingo had known that it was bound to do that. It's what timers do. It had been getting ready to do it for five minutes.

Still, he didn't want it to happen right then, not when he was just getting started on some things he really wanted to say.

"I was just going to say," he went on manfully, "that your letters are wonderful. I've almost got the last one memorized."

Melissa was silent for a moment, and then she said, "Well, I guess we have to say good-bye."

"I guess so."

". . . Good-bye . . . Bingo . . ."

The words were spoken with such reluctance that they seemed to linger in the A T & T lines. He heard Melissa take a breath, and for one tremulous moment, Bingo thought she was going to add the words, ". . . gypsy lover."

He waited, giving her a chance to add that or anything else. But she didn't.

Bingo smiled. Actually he was not completely sorry to see his brief, turbulent days as a gypsy lover come to an end.

"Good-bye, Melissa."

There was one more silence, and Bingo seemed to inhale it. It was as if this silence would have to last him for a lifetime, for eternity, maybe even infinity.

Then Bingo Brown hung up the phone.